Check out what RT Book Reviews *is saying about Rhonda Nelson's heroes in—and out of—uniform!*

Letters from Home
"This highly romantic tale is filled with emotion and wonderful characters. It's a heart-melting romance."

The Soldier
"Wonderfully written and heart-stirring, the story flies by to the deeply satisfying ending."

The Hell-Raiser
"A highly entertaining story that has eccentric secondary characters, hot sex and a heartwarming romance."

The Loner
"A highly romantic story with two heartwarming characters and a surprise ending."

The Ranger
"Well plotted and wickedly sexy, this one's got it all—including a completely scrumptious hero. A keeper."

Blaze

Dear Reader,

While other women might think immediately of romance on Valentine's Day, I don't—I think of chocolate. After nearly twenty years together my husband knows that I don't require dinner out or a box of fancy truffles. Though I've sampled Godiva, Ghirardelli, See's, Whitman's and various other chocolates, nothing tastes as good to me as plain old Hershey's. It's simple, delicious and in that sweet little kiss form? Ah...bliss. And speaking of kisses, the hero in this book certainly knows how to do that well.

Former ranger Jackson Oak Martin is as big, steady and strong as the tree he's named after. But when being too near an exploding bomb renders him partially deaf in one ear, Jack knows that his career in the military is over. When he's recommended for a position at Ranger Security, Jack is unquestionably relieved. Only his first assignment results in forced proximity with pastry chef Mariette Levine and involves catching a "Butter Bandit." Jack can't help but wonder what the hell he's gotten into. Particularly when he becomes obsessed with getting into her....

As always, thanks so much for picking up my books! I am so very thankful for my readers and love hearing from them, so be sure to follow me on Twitter @RhondaRNelson, like me on Facebook and look for upcoming releases and news on my website, ReadRhondaNelson.com.

Happy reading!

Rhonda

Rhonda Nelson

THE KEEPER

Harlequin®

TORONTO NEW YORK LONDON
AMSTERDAM PARIS SYDNEY HAMBURG
STOCKHOLM ATHENS TOKYO MILAN MADRID
PRAGUE WARSAW BUDAPEST AUCKLAND

Recycling programs
for this product may
not exist in your area.

ISBN-13: 978-0-373-79668-7

THE KEEPER

ABOUT THE AUTHOR

A Waldenbooks bestselling author, two-time RITA® Award nominee and *RT Book Reviews* Reviewers' Choice nominee, Rhonda Nelson writes hot romantic comedy for the Harlequin Blaze line and other Harlequin imprints. With more than twenty-five published books to her credit and many more coming down the pike, she's thrilled with her career and enjoys dreaming up her characters and manipulating the worlds they live in. In addition to a writing career, she has a husband, two adorable kids, a black Lab and a beautiful bichon frise. She and her family make their chaotic but happy home in a small town in northern Alabama. She loves to hear from her readers, so be sure and check her out at www.readrhondanelson.com.

Books by Rhonda Nelson

Prologue

"WHAT ABOUT YOU, OAK?" PFC Heath Johnson asked. "What do you want in a woman?"

Doing a routine sweep through his little portion of Baghdad, Major Jackson Oak Martin was only half listening to his fellow comrades enumerate what qualities their ideal woman would possess. He'd been through this area countless times over the past few months and was familiar with every pile of garbage, every mate-less shoe, every blown-out window. He carefully scanned the area ahead, every sense tingling.

Something had changed.

"Eyes out, guys," Jack told them, slowing down as the hair on the back of his neck prickled uneasily. "I'm pulling a weird vibe."

"Bullshit," PFC Chris Fulmer scoffed, seemingly annoyed and bored, his usual mood. "It's the same old, same old here, Major. Nothing's happened in weeks in this area. I don't know why we can't move on," he continued to predictably complain. He grunted. "Ignorant-ass waste of time, if you ask me." He shot a grin at Johnson and pulled a cocky shrug. "You want to know what *I* want in a woman, Johnson? It's simple enough." He made an obscene gesture.

The group laughed and Jack quickly quieted them, growing increasingly uncomfortable. Dammit, he knew something was different. Could feel it. He looked left, then right, along both sides of the cluttered abandoned street. He scanned the rooftops and windows, the blown-out cars and debris. On the surface everything appeared undisturbed, innocuous even, but every iota of intuition he possessed was telling him that it wasn't, that something—however small—had been altered.

And the small things were just as capable of getting them killed as the big things were.

"You're a shallow bastard, you know that, Fulmer?" Johnson told him.

The young Nebraskan was as wholesome as the farm he'd grown up on, intelligent and wise beyond his years, and had quickly become one of Jack's favorites.

A dreamy expression drifted over Johnson's face. "I just want a woman who can cook. One who knows that potatoes don't come out of a box and are better mashed, with gravy. One who knows how to fry chick—"

A blast to their immediate right cut off the rest of what Johnson was going to say, along with his legs.

Jack felt the power of the detonation roll over his body—a terrible shock of pain to his right ear—and felt himself fly through the air and land hard on his left side. He couldn't catch his breath—it had been knocked out of him—and struggled to force the immediate panic aside. Debris and dust clouded his vision, making his eyes water and sting. He lifted his head, saw Johnson shaking uncontrollably on the ground, part of Fulmer's skull clasped in his own hand, and Wilson and Manning were both bleeding from various parts of their bodies.

Oh, Jesus...

He immediately radioed for help, then, heartsick and terrified, lunged into action, crawling with more speed than grace to Johnson's side.

The boy's big blue eyes were wide with shock, and his mouth worked up and down. He grabbed Jack's sleeve and yanked him down. His ashen lips moved shakily, but no sound emerged.

"Medic's on the way," Jack assured him, tearing bits of fabric from the edge of his jacket to fashion a makeshift tourniquet. So much blood, he thought, working frantically, his hands slippery with it. It was a mortal wound, he knew—he was familiar enough with war to know that—but he had to try, had to help. This was Johnson, dammit, his friend.

Johnson writhed and tried to bat his hands away, but Jack roughly pushed him back down. "I gotta do it," he told him, feeling his insides vibrate with dread. "I know it hurts like a bitch, but just stay strong, buddy." Jack could feel his heart thundering in his chest, the tremor in his fingers, a trickle of something wet and sticky running down his neck.

Before he could attach the second tourniquet, Johnson jerked him around hard, his pale, freckled face a mask of pain and desperation. He kept talking—seemed to be desperately trying to impart something significant—but his lips only moved. Seemingly frustrated when Jack didn't respond, Johnson tried harder, appearing to scream. He said whatever it was again, gave him another little shake, then fell back against the ground once more. His eyes drifted shut.

Oh, no. No, no, no.

"Johnson," Jack said, grabbing the boy's shoulder. "Stay with me, Johnson. Dammit, don't—"

A hand suddenly landed on his shoulder and Jack whirled and struck out, sending the medic sprawling. A second medic was right behind the first and a helicopter had landed in the street fifty yards from where they were located. Jack watched the blades whirl, belatedly noting the lack of sound. He frowned, his gaze darting from one person to the next, watched their lips move, saw the action and reaction.

Dread ballooned in his belly and his heart began to race even faster as the unhappy truth slammed into him.

PFC Heath Johnson had just uttered his last words…to a man who couldn't hear them.

1

Six months later...

PERHAPS BECAUSE HE WAS now partially deaf in his right ear, former-Ranger Jack Martin was certain he had to have heard his new employers incorrectly. He chuckled uneasily.

"The Butter Bandit?"

Brian Payne—one of the three founding members of the infamous Ranger Security Company—nodded and shot a look at fellow partner Guy McCann. "That's what Guy has dubbed him and, I'm sad to say, it's stuck."

Jamie Flanagan, who rounded out the triumvirate, flashed a what-the-hell sort of grin. "You've got to admit that it has a certain ring to it." He pulled a face. "Besides, other than a few éclairs, cookies and bear claws, butter is the *only* thing this thief is stealing."

How…bizarre, Jack thought. He was most definitely a fan of butter—who didn't like it melting on a pile of pancakes or slathering it over a hot roll? He had fond memories of making it himself with nothing more than a little heavy whipping cream in an old mason jar and shaking it up until his arms were tired, the unmistakable "plop" against the side of the jar, signaling it was done. He'd learned the trick from his grandmother, who'd been more butter obsessed than Paula Deen.

But he couldn't imagine even her *stealing* the stuff. It boggled the mind.

"Have there been any other butter thefts in the area?" Jack asked, trying to get his mind around the idea. Not a question he would have ever anticipated coming out of his mouth, but then again nothing about his recent life was anything he'd anticipated.

Leaving the military before retirement had never been in any plans he'd made—unless it had been in a pine box, which he'd been fully prepared to do—much less moving to anywhere other than Pennyroyal, North Carolina, upon retirement. He'd actually purchased property next to his parents there in his little hometown and had been toying with various house plans for years. Just something else he'd need to rethink at a later date.

At present he was just glad to have a job, to have had an alternative to sitting behind a desk for the rest of his career. The mere idea made him feel claustrophobic, hemmed in. While Jack knew there were many powerful men who did their best work from an office, he was not one of those men. He liked to *move,* needed some sort of physical action to coincide with his strategy.

Of course, sitting still had never been easy for him. Even in kindergarten his poor teacher had had to mark a square—with duct tape, the wonder material—on the floor around his desk to keep him there. If he came out of the "box" without permission, then he lost time on the playground.

While other people might think she was being cruel or unreasonable, Jack knew she'd had good reason. He'd given the poor woman sheer hell, had been virtually incapable of sitting still for any length of time. He could hear her, understand and learn without looking at her—while looking at something else or doing something else, like playing with a toy truck, for instance, he thought with a mental smile—but he hadn't realized until much later that other people didn't learn that way. With maturity had come discipline, but the underlying need to move was always itching just beneath the surface.

Even now.

That's what had made the military so perfect for him. Action, reaction, strategy, purpose. It had been the ideal fit. And while Ranger Security wasn't the military, it was run by former Rangers—men like himself—and, though he fully anticipated an adjustment, he knew he was up to the task. He almost smiled.

Even catching a butter thief, of all things, which was evidently going to be his first assignment for the company.

"No," Guy replied to his question. "No other butter thefts in the area. Mariette's store is the only one that's been targeted. We've canvassed the area just to be sure."

"Under normal circumstances we wouldn't be taking this on at all, but after last night we just can't sit back and do nothing," Payne said, his tone grim. "Mariette's more than a local business owner—she's a good friend, as well." He gestured to the other two men. "She's provided many a cup of coffee, breakfasts and snacks for us over the past three years. She's hosted our kids' birthday parties—"

"For which we are eternally thankful," Jamie added with a significant grimace.

"—and her shop is right here on our block."

In other words, *their* turf, *their* friend.

Jack had actually noticed the little bakery when he first arrived here in Atlanta a week ago. It was a pretty redbrick with whimsical window boxes stuffed with yellow and lavender mums. "Raw Sugar" was written in fancy script from a sign shaped like a three-tiered cake. There'd been a teenage girl with Down syndrome sweeping the walk out in front and she'd looked so happy it had brought a smile to his lips.

"What happened last night?" Jack asked, a bad feeling settling in his gut.

The three men shared a dark look. "Mariette heard a noise and went downstairs to investigate—"

"She lives above the shop," Jamie interjected, pausing to take a pull from his drink.

"—and interrupted the guy. Instead of running like a normal criminal who'd been caught, he picked up a dough roller and hurled it at her." Payne's voice lowered ominously. "It caught her behind the ear and knocked her out cold."

Damn, Jack thought, anger immediately bolting through him. He'd like to take a dough roller to the jackass for throwing it at a woman. No wonder they'd decided to intervene. Even though she'd been assaulted this still wasn't a case that was going to get high priority to an overworked local P.D. His grandfather, father and sister had all worn the uniform, so he should know. He'd thwarted tradition when he'd traded the badge for a pair of dog tags, a fact his father never failed to remind him of when he went home. Good-naturedly, of course, but Jack knew his decision to not follow in the "family business" had stuck in his father's craw.

"Do you have any idea what he's looking for?" Jack asked. "Aside from butter, that is?" There was no way in hell this was just about butter. If that were the case, their thief would be hitting multiple businesses, not just Raw Sugar.

Jamie shook his head and released a mighty sigh. "Not a damned clue."

"That's where you're going to come in," Payne told him. "She needs protection, obviously, but more than that we need to know what this guy's after. You find the motive and you'll resolve the threat."

He certainly couldn't fault that logic. He had no idea where in the hell he was going to start looking for motive—with Mariette, he supposed—but otherwise this didn't seem as though it was going to be too involved and shouldn't interfere with his other… project.

"Because the thief hasn't struck during the day while the shop is open, we're assuming that she's in less danger at that point. We're putting Charlie in under the guise of 'helping out' until Mariette closes, which will free you up to investigate during those hours and then cover protection at night, when he's most likely to strike again."

The mention of his sister, Charlie—who was the first female nonmilitary, non-Ranger employee hired on by the company—brought a smile to his lips. He and his sister had always been tight and, if there were a silver lining at all to his impromptu career change, it was that he'd get to see her on a regular basis. He'd actually moved into his new brother-in-law's former apartment here in the building.

When the idea of coming on board with Ranger Security after the accident had first been mentioned, it was ultimately Jay who had convinced him that it would be the right move. The first look at the "boardroom" with its high-end electronics and toys, pool table and kitchenette—complete with its own candy counter—had been proof enough before anything else had been discussed. Between the unbelievable benefits package—the salary, the hardware, the furnished apartment—and the familiar camaraderie of former battle-worn soldiers, he knew that he'd been lucky to find a place where he felt sure he would eventually feel at home. He grimaced.

At the moment, even home didn't feel like home.

But how could it, really? After what had happened in Baghdad? An image of Johnson's frantic, desperate face loomed large in his mind's eye—the dirt and the blood—and with effort, he forced the vision to recede.

For the moment, anyway. Until he could properly analyze it again. Sheer torture, but it had to be done. He would keep analyzing it for the rest of his life if he had to. He owed the kid no less.

Typically when Jack returned stateside it was to a big party and lots of fanfare. He was the only son and frankly, as the former all-star quarterback for the high-school football team, Pennyroyal's golden boy. He was generally met with a cry of delight, a hearty slap on the back, a little nudge-nudge wink-wink and a free drink.

The tone had been decidedly different this time.

The smiles had been pitying and bittersweet, the slaps on the back held a tinge of regret and finality and, because he'd been wounded, there hadn't been a party.

It was just as well. He hadn't felt like celebrating.

Payne handed him a thin file. He'd already given him a laptop, a Glock, the permit to carry concealed and the keys to his furnished and fully stocked apartment. Brian Payne had thought of everything, but then, that's what one expected out of a man dubbed "the Specialist" by his comrades, Jack thought, surveying the seemingly unflappable former Ranger. His gaze briefly shifted to the other two men.

With a purported genius-level IQ and an equal amount of brawn, Jamie Flanagan had been the ultimate player until he met and married Colonel Carl Garrett's granddaughter, and Guy McCann's ability to skate the fine edge of recklessness and never tip over into stupidity was still locker room lore.

He couldn't be working with finer men. Or *woman,* he belatedly added, knowing his sister wouldn't appreciate the unintended slight.

"Mariette is expecting you," Payne told him. He hesitated and, for whatever reason, that small delay made Jack's belly clench. He glanced at his partners, whose expressions suddenly became mildly humorous, then found Jack's once more. "While she appreciates our help, she's not exactly happy about the way in which we're providing it."

Jack felt his lips slide into a smirk. In other words, she didn't want him to spend the night with her.

In truth, he wasn't exactly looking forward to spending the night at her place, either. He was still having damned nightmares and didn't relish the idea of having to explain himself. Besides, cohabitating with a woman for any reason made his feet itch and triggered the urge to bolt.

Irrational? Probably.

But he'd given it a go with his former college sweetheart and that had ended…disastrously.

Both the relationship and the cohabitation.

Who knew that having only one foot of five in closet space would irritate him to no end? Or that the way she ground her teeth at night would feel like psychological torture? Or that when he'd rebelled against the minimal closet space she'd thrown all of his shit out into the yard and set it on fire with charcoal starter and a flame thrower? Jack frowned.

In retrospect she'd been a little unbalanced—brought a whole new meaning to the phrase "crazy sex"—but the lesson had been learned all the same. He liked his own space. He liked his own bed. He liked making his own rules. As such, he didn't do sleepovers. When the goal was met—typically a little mutually satisfying sex with no strings or expectations—he ultimately retreated to his own place.

And planned to *always* retreat to his own space.

Jack didn't know when he'd made the conscious decision to never marry, but when his mother had concluded her I'm-so-glad-you're-home speech with a succinct nod and a "Now you can settle down and get married," he'd mentally recoiled at the thought.

The reaction had been jarring and, even more so, unexpected.

In all truth, he'd never really given much thought to the idea of marriage. He'd been busy building a career he loved, distilling the values he'd always appreciated—courage, honor, love of country, being a man who didn't just give his word, but kept it, one who followed through and always got the job done. He worked hard on the battlefield and played hard off it.

Life, full *friggin'* throttle, unencumbered by any other ties.

And he'd liked it that way.

He hadn't realized exactly how much until after the accident, when everything in his world had shifted.

Losing Fulmer and Johnson had certainly changed him—death had a way of doing that to a person—and the hearing loss had ultimately cost him a career he'd loved, but he'd be damned before he'd give up the only part of himself he'd managed to hold on to. He was still Jackson Oak Martin and, though this life was a stark departure from the one he left behind, he'd figure out a way to make it work.

Because that's what he did.

And the alternative was simply unacceptable.

And, friend of Ranger Security or not, this Mariette person was just going to have to deal with it because he had a damned butter thief to find.

PAYNE WATCHED THEIR newest recruit leave the boardroom and then turned to his partners and quirked a brow. "That went better than I expected," he said. "A lesser man might have balked at catching a butter bandit."

Guy pushed up from the leather recliner he'd been slouched in and grabbed a pool stick. He carefully lined up his shot and sent the number three into the corner pocket. "He's certainly the most determined man we've ever brought on board, I'll say that." He frowned thoughtfully. "And not twitchy, but…barely contained."

Payne had noted that, as well. Jack Martin didn't shift in his seat, avoid eye contact, tap his fingers or his feet—didn't fidget at all, actually—and yet, like a thoroughbred waiting behind the gate, the energy was there. Banked anticipation. Bridled action.

Having joined Guy, Jamie took a shot at the nine and missed. He swore and absently chalked his cue. "Charlie said that the only thing that made leaving the military bearable for him was the job he knew would be waiting here."

Payne could definitely see where that would be the case and Colonel Carl Garrett had seconded Charlie's opinion. According to the Colonel, before the incident in Baghdad, Jack Martin had been rapidly rising through the ranks, on the verge of lieutenant-colonel status. He was well-favored, determined and dedicated. He was a man who had been in love with his career and, though he could have stayed on in another capacity within the military, he couldn't have continued along the same path.

It said a lot about his character that he was willing to blaze a new one.

"You can barely see the hearing aid," Jamie remarked. "I wouldn't have noticed it at all if I hadn't been looking for it."

The blast that had killed two of his men and injured two others had shattered Jack's eardrum so thoroughly that he'd needed multiple surgeries to repair it. As injuries went, he was damned lucky, but it had to have been an adjustment, all the same.

"Has Charlie found out why he's taking the lip-reading classes yet?" Guy asked.

"No." And he wished their curious, master hacker would leave that well enough alone. Everyone was entitled to a few secrets and, for whatever reason, Payne got the impression that the one Jack was trying to keep was as painful as it was significant.

Charlie digging around in something her brother had decided was private wasn't going to endear her to him if he found out. Of course, Jack probably knew Charlie well enough to know that she couldn't resist a mystery and considered very little privileged information sacred. He almost grinned.

It was part of the reason they'd hired her, after all.

"It doesn't make sense," Jamie chimed in. "He can hear. Why would he need to know how to read lips?"

Payne shrugged. "I'm sure he has his reasons."

Jamie took another pull from his drink and settled a hip against the pool table. "I just hope that Mariette doesn't make things too difficult for him. We're *helping* her, for heaven's sake." He shook his head. "Why is being grateful a concept women struggle with?"

Payne felt his lips twist. "She didn't *ask* for our help."

Jamie blinked. "That's my point exactly. She didn't *have* to ask."

"I don't think it's the help that she objects to, per se," Guy remarked, his lips sliding into a smile. "It's the us not leaving her a choice that's got her back up."

"Charlie said we could have handled it better," Jamie said. He paused thoughtfully and grimaced. "Actually, what she really said is that we were all a bunch of high-handed, knuckle-dragging idiots with the tact of a herd of stampeding elephants. Or something like that."

Payne chuckled. That sounded about right. And he'd never met a woman who liked being told what to do. He frowned thoughtfully.

Mariette certainly wasn't going to be the exception there.

He hoped Jack realized that sooner rather than later.

2

MARIETTE LEVINE WAS IN the process of pulling a red-velvet cupcake from the display case when she heard the bell over the door jingle and saw a pair of impossibly long, jeans-clad legs come into view. They sidled forward in a walk that was so blatantly sexy and loose hipped that she momentarily forgot what she was doing.

A flash of pure sexual heat instantly blazed through her, the sensation so unexpected and shocking she felt her eyes round and her breath catch.

Instead of standing up—which would have been the logical thing to do—for reasons that escaped her, Mariette dropped into a deeper crouch so that she could get a better look at the rest of him. She was *not* hiding, Mariette told herself. She had no reason to hide, even if she would admit to being curiously… alarmed.

How singularly odd.

She had no reason to be alarmed, either, and yet something about the stranger—whose face she hadn't even seen yet—triggered an imminent sense of danger. Not of the axe-murderer variety, but something else…something much more personal. Her racing heart stupidly skipped a beat and her mouth went dry.

Intrigued, her gaze drifted up over his crotch—it had to, dammit, to get to the rest of him—and took a more thorough inventory. He wore an oatmeal-colored cable-knit sweater—oh, how she loved a cable-knit sweater on a man—and a leather bomber jacket that had seen better days. His hands were stuffed into the pockets, his broad shoulders still a bit hunched beneath the cold. He was impossibly… big. Not apish or fat, but tall and lean hipped and muscled in all the right places.

And if his architecture was magnificent, it was nothing compared to the perfect harmony of his face. *Sweet heaven…*

High cheekbones, intriguing hollows, an especially angular, squared-off jaw. His nose was perfectly proportioned and straight, his mouth a little wide and over full. Sleek brows winged over a pair of heavy-lidded, sleepy-looking light eyes—either green or blue, she couldn't tell from this distance, though instinct told her blue.

His hair was a pale golden-blond, parted to the side, almost all one length and hung to just above his collar. He exuded confidence, fearlessness and moved with a casual deliberateness that suggested he was a man who was well aware of his own strength and ability. He didn't merely inhabit a space—he *owned* it.

And she wasn't the only one who'd noticed. Several of her patrons had stopped to look at him—mouths hanging open, forks suspended in midair—and a quick look to her right revealed that her helper, Livvie, had gone stock-still.

"Wow," she heard Livvie breathe, her eyes rounded in wonder. "You're *tall*. Like the corn man, but not green."

Charlie Martin Weatherford, her assigned day-time bodyguard working under the guise of helping out, exited the kitchen and her step momentarily faltered, then a brilliant smile bloomed over her mouth. "'Bout time you got here," she said to the mystery man with a good-natured snort of impatience. "You get lost, big brother?"

Big brother? Mariette felt her eyes widen and the original irrational panic that had sent her pulse racing only a minute before was minimal to the arrhythmia that had set in now. This was Charlie's brother? *This* air-breathing Greek god in a bomber jacket was the man who was going to be spending the night with her until this ignorant dairy thief was caught?

Oh, no. *No, no, no...*

She didn't know why oh-no, but she knew it all the same. Could feel some sort of impending doom with every particle of her being.

She'd been right to be alarmed.

It was self-preservation in its purest form. He was disaster with a tight-assed swagger and she knew herself too well to think he'd be anything other than irresistible. Why couldn't he have been the aging-detective type her too-vivid imagination had conjured up? She peered up at him again and resisted the urge to whimper. No paunch, jowls or receding hairline in sight.

Just six and a half feet of pure masculine temptation.

Livvie looked down at her and smiled. "Look at him, Mariette," she said in a stage whisper, her small, almond-shaped blue eyes alight with wonder. "There's a giant in the shop."

Following Livvie's gaze Charlie looked down at her, as well, and her lips twitched with knowing humor, as though she knew exactly why Mariette was hiding.

"He's not a giant, Livvie," Charlie told her, slinging an arm around the younger girl. "He's just a very tall man."

She looked at Mariette, arched a questioning brow and mouthed, "Corn man?"

Very reluctantly, Mariette rose, mentally braced herself and turned to meet Charlie's brother. She could hear her heart thundering in her ears and her mouth had yet to recover any of its lost moisture. A breathless sort of anticipation gripped her as she looked up.

She'd been right, she discovered—his eyes were blue. And not just any shade of blue. *French blue.*

Her favorite, naturally.

Though she was utterly certain the earth hadn't moved, Mariette felt it all the same. The soles of her feet practically vibrated from the imaginary vibration. The entire room, with the exception of the space he occupied, seemed to shimmy and shake. Her lungs went on temporary strike and a hot flush rushed over her skin, as though she'd been hit with an invisible blowtorch from one end of her body to the other. Her toes actually curled in her shoes.

Remarkable.

At twenty-seven, Mariette had met many good-looking men and knew enough about sexual attraction to recognize it. But this was unmistakably different. It wasn't a dawning awareness of an attractive man.

This was a bare-knuckle sucker punch of lust—purely visceral—and undeniably the most potent reaction she'd ever had to a man. It was the sort of attraction that was rhapsodized in lyric and verse, secured the human race, rendered reason and logic useless, made one stupid.

It was the sort that could ruin a person.

But not her, dammit. Geez Lord, hadn't she just learned her lesson? What had Nathanial been if not a warning? Aside from a cheating, dishonest little bastard, anyway? To think that she'd been seriously considering marrying him.

Just like all the other men she'd misjudged—and, lamentably, there'd been many—on the surface Nathaniel had seemed like a perfect catch. He was a successful architect working for a local, prestigious firm. He'd stopped by her shop for three solid months, asking her out every single time he came through the door until she said yes. She'd been flattered and she'd liked the fact that he hadn't been a quitter, that he'd been persistent. She'd thought that, in him, she'd finally found *the one*. A real, stand-up guy who genuinely loved her the same way that her mother always had—*unconditionally*.

In reality he just hadn't been used to anyone telling him no. Come to find out she hadn't been the only person he'd been pursuing relentlessly—there'd been several others.

And when she'd caught him getting blown by the plant-watering girl—whose dirty feet still haunted her—at his office, she'd been shocked, humiliated, angry and hurt. The pain hadn't come just from the betrayal, which had been devastating enough—it had come from not being able to trust her own judgment. With previous guys she'd had an inkling of disquiet, an intuitive niggle of doubt that she'd ultimately ignored. Smooth-talking, greasy Nathaniel had slipped completely under her radar. And he'd had a crooked dick, too, Mariette thought. If nothing else, that should have clued her in.

Note to self: Never trust a man with a crooked dick.

To complicate matters, despite her telling him to go play in traffic, he still hadn't learned to accept no for an answer and continued to drop by in the slower hours and try to convince her to take him back. She mentally snorted.

As if.

Fool me once, shame on you. Fool me twice, shame on me. She might not always get things right, but she was a firm believer in education by experience…and that was one she didn't want to repeat.

Mariette steeled herself against her newest battle of temptation. "Are you in any way related to the Jolly Green Giant, Mr. Martin?" Mariette asked him, determined to get control of herself. He was only a man, after all. A mouthwatering, bone-melting, sigh-inducing, lady-bits-quivering specimen of one, yes.

But still just a man. And those were supposed to be off-limits, at least until she figured out just what it was exactly she wanted in one and how to recognize it.

He chewed the inside of his cheek as if to hide a smile. "Not that I'm aware of, no."

"Sorry, Livvie," Mariette told her with a wince. "He's not a giant."

Livvie looked unconvinced, but beamed up at him regardless. "It's all right," she said, smiling shyly. "I like him anyway."

Seemingly charmed, he extended his hand to her. "I'm Jack," he said. "It's a pleasure to meet you."

Livvie giggled delightedly and fingered the Hello Kitty necklace around her throat. "You're nice." She leaned over to Mariette and whispered loudly in her ear—loud was Livvie's only volume—"He's a gold."

Jack's expression became puzzled, but he didn't question it. Livvie said she saw people in colors and was forever telling Mariette which color various people were. She even kept a small color wheel in her apron pocket so that she could easily locate the right shade. Mariette, she'd said, was a lavender. Charlie, a fuchsia. If memory served, Jack was her first gold. Interesting…

Mariette wasn't surprised that Livvie could so clearly see auras. She was as pure of heart as it was possible to be and Mariette liked to think that the gift had been given to her as a means of protection, a way to recognize the good from the bad, and had even seen the girl retreat away from those whose "color" wasn't right.

Would that her mother had had the same sort of gift.

At any rate, Jack Martin had passed her "Livvie

test" and that said something about him. You could
tell a lot about a person by the way they reacted
to someone different from themselves and Livvie
was about as different from Jack Martin as it was
possible to be. She was small and round-faced with
the short fingers and lower IQ that marked her as a
person with Down syndrome.

The majority of Mariette's customers treated
Livvie with the sort of care and respect someone
with the purest heart deserved—children, in particular, were drawn to her—and anyone who didn't
treat her well wasn't anyone who was welcome in
her shop.

Born to a mother with Down's who'd been taken
advantage of by a male caregiver, Mariette had a
unique connection to the condition and had been em-
ploying workers with Down's since she first opened
her doors four years ago.

If she'd learned anything from her mother it had
been that everyone—no matter how different—
wanted to be needed, to be useful, to have a bit of
independence. There wasn't a day that went by that
she didn't miss her and not a day that went by that
she didn't want to hurt the father who'd abused her
trusting spirit.

Bastard.

He'd served eighteen months for what he'd done
to her mother and then promptly fled the state. Mariette kept tabs on him, though, and directed every

new employer to his sex-offender status. She inwardly grinned. He never kept a job for very long. He struggled and, though it might be small of her, she thought it was fitting. He deserved that and a lot worse if you asked her.

The idea that his evil blood actually ran in her veins was something she'd struggled with for years, at times even making her physically ill. But her mother's was there, too, and Mariette liked to think that her mom's especially good blood had somehow canceled out that of her father's. Weird? Yes. But she'd never been destined for normal.

Normal was boring.

Her gaze drifted fondly over her dear helper and she smiled. Livvie had been with her for several months now and was doing remarkably well. She loved manning the case and *adored* sweeping. She helped with the birthday parties and refilled drinks and every tip that went into the jar was hers to keep. Which was just as well since the bulk of her check went to fund her Hello Kitty obsession. Her most recent purchase was the watch that encircled her wrist.

"Can I get you something?" Mariette asked Jack, gesturing to the display case.

He hesitated.

"He has a fondness for carrot cake," Charlie interjected slyly.

Mariette shot him a droll look and selected the

cupcake in question. It had been her aunt's recipe—
and was one of her favorites, as well. Oh, hell. Who
was she kidding? Everything in this shop was her
favorite, otherwise she didn't take the time to make
or stock it. Food was a passionate business and if she
couldn't get excited about it—if it didn't make her
palate sing—then she didn't bother. Better to have
fewer phenomenal items on her menu than dozens
of mediocre ones.

Also something she'd learned from her Aunt
Marianne, who'd not only helped raise her, but had
taught her to bake, as well. Some of her fondest
memories were in the kitchen with her aunt and her
mom, cracking eggs, stirring batter, the scent of vanilla in the air.

She popped the dessert onto a little antique plate
along with a linen napkin and handed it to him. Seconds later Livvie had put a glass of tea in his hand.
She'd added two lemons and a cherry, which told
Mariette just how much Livvie thought of him. She
only put cherries in the drinks of her favorite people.
He nodded approvingly at her and shot her a wink,
making her giggle with pleasure once more.

His blue gaze shifted to Mariette and that direct
regard made her more than a little light-headed. "Is
there somewhere we can talk?" he asked, lifting a
golden brow. "I've got a few questions."

Mariette took a bracing breath and prepared herself for imminent humiliation. She couldn't imag-

ine anything more mortifying than telling this man about her butter problems.

MARIETTE LEVINE WAS NOT at all what he'd expected, Jack thought broodingly as he followed her back to the kitchen. Actually, he hadn't really given any thought to what she might be like, so that wasn't precisely true. But—his gaze drifted over her petite curvy frame, lingering on her especially ripe heart-shaped ass—*this* woman wouldn't have been it.

In the first place, Mariette sounded like an old-fashioned name, so he'd imagined a more mature woman. Oh, hell, who was he kidding? He'd thought she'd be old. Which was ridiculous, really. Not all bakeries were owned by plump grandmas in floral aprons, though for reasons that escaped him that was the image that had leapt immediately to mind.

He estimated this particular baker to be in her mid- to late-twenties. In the second place… Well, there wasn't really a second place, though logic told him there should have been. And a third and a fourth and a fifth, for that matter. Furthermore, he felt as though he should have been warned, but couldn't come up with a logical reason for that, either.

What would they have said? *Oh, by the way, Mariette's young and hot with the most unusual gray eyes you'll ever see? That long mink-colored hair will incite the urge to wrap it around your fist and drag her up against you? And her mouth…* Jack swallowed thickly. A much fuller lower lip, a distinct bow in the upper and a perpetual tilt at the corner that suggested she was always enjoying a private joke. It was sinfully sensual nestled between her pert little nose and small pointy chin.

She wasn't merely pretty or beautiful—though those adjectives would apply, as well—but there was something *more* there. Something much more substantial and compelling, and the bizarre tightening in his chest that had occurred when her gaze had met his had been nothing short of terrifying.

Jack wasn't accustomed to being afraid of anything other than failure, so discovering that a woman could incite the feeling was a bit unsettling.

Honestly, when she'd risen up from behind that counter he couldn't have been more surprised if he'd been hit between the eyes with a two-by-four. He'd damned-near *staggered*.

From a single look.

Like a tsunami running headlong into a hurricane.

If he had any brains at all he'd turn around and leave, Jack thought. He'd walk right back up the block to Ranger Security and tell them that they needed to put someone else on this particular case, to give him another one. But short of a natural disaster metaphor, how in the hell could he explain his reasoning?

How could he tell them that she made his gut

clench and his dick hard? That intuition told him he was headed into uncharted emotional and sexual territory and, weak as it might sound, he wasn't altogether certain he'd be able to control himself? That something about her scared the hell out of him? *A girl?*

How galling.

He couldn't tell them that, dammit. He needed this job, had to make it work. He couldn't bail on the first damned assignment.

And as much as he was compelled to flee, there was an opposite force equally as strong that was drawing him toward her, intriguing him, transfixing him, and between the two he was stuck, immobile and powerless.

Another punch of fear landed in his gut.

Mariette gestured toward a small table, indicating a seat and she took the one opposite. A couple of women worked at a large stainless-steel table drizzling icing over pastries and the scent of yeast and sugar hung in the air, reminding him of Christmastime at home, when his mother made her famous cinnamon rolls. Every surface gleamed beneath the large, overhead lights. An old wooden ladder outfitted with metal hooks was suspended from the ceiling and held a variety of pots and tongs of varying degrees and sizes.

A peg board had been anchored to one long wall and held dozens of bowls, measuring cups, couplings and icing tips. Fresh flowers sat in old, blue Mason jars on the back windowsill and yet another board— this one a dry erase with what he could only assume were orders—took up another wall. The space was small—narrow like the building—but had been maximized with state-of-the-art appliances and sheer ingenuity.

He was impressed and said as much. "This is a great setup," he told her.

Seemingly pleased, she smiled and tucked a long strand of hair behind her ear. "It was a lot of trial and error in the beginning, but I think I've finally got everything organized in the most efficient manner."

He took a bite of his cupcake and savored the spices against his tongue. It was moist and flavorful, and the icing was perfect—not too sweet, with just the right cream cheese to sugar ratio. Not everyone got that part right, but she'd mastered it.

"And you live upstairs?"

She nodded, swept an imaginary crumb from the table. "I do. I keep long hours and economically, it just made more sense." A wry grin curled her lips. "I've got one mortgage as opposed to two."

Definitely savvy. Sexy, smart and she could cook, too. He hoped to hell he discovered a flaw soon. A hairy mole or a snorting laugh. Anything to derail this horribly inconvenient attraction.

"And when did you notice that someone was stealing your butter? When did the Butter Bandit first strike?"

Looking adorably mortified, she blushed prettily, a wash of bright pink beneath creamy skin. "Three days ago," she said. "At first I just thought one of the girls—possibly Livvie—had moved it from one part of the walk-in to the other. It's a big space and I keep it well stocked. I only use organic products and everything has to be fresh, otherwise the quality isn't up to par."

He could certainly taste the difference. "But it hadn't been moved?"

She shook her head. "No. And more than half of it had been taken."

"And how much is half?"

She chewed the inside of her cheek, speculating. "Roughly thirty pounds."

Jack felt his eyes widen. *"Thirty pounds?"*

She laughed, the sound husky and melodic. *Definitely not a snorter, then. Damn.*

"I typically use between sixty and seventy pounds of butter a week." She gestured to five-gallon lidded buckets beneath the main work station. "That's flour and sugar. And that smaller fridge against the wall? That one holds nothing but eggs."

Good Lord. He'd had no idea. Of course, since he'd never made any sort of dessert in his life that didn't come out of a box and require that he add only water, why would he?

But thirty pounds of butter? Who in the hell would steal *thirty* pounds of butter? To what purpose? For what possible use?

And they'd come back for more and *attacked* her for it.

"Who supplies your butter?" Jack wanted to know. It seemed like the best place to start. Perhaps there was something special about Mariette's butter. Maybe it was made from goat's milk or only harvested during the full moon. Maybe it was intentional butter, much like that Intentional Chocolate he'd gotten in a care package from his mother last year. Supposedly, it had been infused with good intentions by experienced meditators. Enchanted butter, he thought, tamping down the absurdity of the situation. He'd be damned if he knew.

But it was his job to find out, he reminded himself.

"Jefferson's Dairy just north of Marietta," she told him. "They furnish my eggs and milk, as well."

Jack nodded and pushed up from his chair, determined to get started. The sooner he figured this out the better. Besides, one of the ladies had fired up a mixer and the whine was wreaking hell with his hearing aid. For the most part, the little miracle piece could almost make him forget that he needed it at all, but then a certain sound would set it off and he'd be reminded all over again. For the most part, he'd learned to cope with the "disability"—and knew that he'd gotten off easy in comparison to most other war-sustained injuries—but it was still jarring, nonetheless. An instant reminder of what he'd lost, an automatic, haunting flashback to Johnson's desperate face. He gave himself a mental shake, forcing himself to focus on the task at hand.

The bleeding, bedamned Butter Bandit.

The dairy sounded as good as any place to begin. "I'm sure that Payne has called them already, but I want to go out there and do a little poking around."

She stood, as well. "Of course."

"What time do you close?"

"Six."

He nodded once. "Then I'll be back at six."

A fleeting look of irritation and panic raced across her fine features so fast he was almost inclined to believe he'd imagined it.

But he hadn't. For whatever reason—insanity, probably—that gave him an irrational burst of pleasure. The whole misery-loved-company bit? he wondered. Or was it something else? Was the idea of rattling her cage the way she was rattling his the culprit? He inwardly smiled.

It was fair, if nothing else, Jack decided.

A thought struck. "Did you get any sort of look at the guy at all before he threw the dough roller?"

The mere thought of it—of her being hurt—brought on the instant urge to hit something. Preferably the asshole who threw the dough roller at her.

What the hell was wrong with people anyway? Jack thought.

She smiled sadly and shook her head. "He was tall and skinny," she said. "He was wearing a hoodie and it was dark. I—"

"No worries," he told her. "I'll get him."

And when he did he was going to think of new and unusual ways to use that damned dough roller on *him*.

3

BOBBY RAY BISHOP KEPT his head down and his ball cap pulled low as he made his way past Mariette Levine's bakery, but darted a quick look through the shop window all the same. The little slow girl was there, as usual. She never failed to give him a hug when he came by with a delivery—he relished those hugs because they were the only ones he ever got. He hadn't been given a pat on the head, much less a hug, since he was eight, so it had been a shock at first, but a pleasant one. No sign of Mariette, but another woman with shoulder-length dark hair whom he'd never seen before was behind the counter. His heart kicked into a faster rhythm.

A new person working in Mariette's place?

Shit, shit, shit. His hands began to shake. He must have hurt her bad, Bobby Ray thought. Could have even killed her.

He hurried past and rounded the corner, then

leaned against the wall of the next building and pulled long, deep breaths into his seizing lungs. Panic and nausea clawed their way up his throat and his nose poured snot, which he dashed away with the back of his hand. He felt tears burn the backs of his lids and blinked them away, determined not to cry. When had crying ever done him any good anyway? Just earned him a backhand against the face or a knock upside the head.

Or worse.

I ain't raisin' no sissy boy, his father had always said. *You gonna cry, then I'll give you something to cry about.*

And he had.

God help him, what was he going to do? He'd been sleeping in his car for days, moving from one place to another to stay at least a step ahead of Uncle Mackie. He snorted. Uncle Mackie wasn't his real uncle, of course. He probably wasn't anyone's uncle at all, but the name had come up at some point or another and stuck, and now it had the power to make him quiver with fear and practically piss himself.

Bobby Ray had lived in fear most of his life and he was sick to death of it.

Uncle Mackie was a bookie and, after a few ill-advised bets plus interest plus whatever "fee" Mackie decided he owed, Bobby Ray was into him for four grand.

It might as well be a million.

He didn't make enough at the dairy to come anywhere near that amount and didn't have anything of value to sell. At nineteen he had a beat-up fifteen-year-old Buick with a salvage title, and lived in a pay-by-the-week motel room. Better than foster care, which he'd ultimately aged out of, thank God, but certainly not the high life, either.

He wiped his nose on the sleeve of his shirt and looked enviously at passersby with their fancy clothes, smartphones and gold watches. He'd bet none of these people had a clue about how people like him lived. Eating microwave mac and cheese every night for dinner, waiting for an empty dryer with a few minutes left on the timer at the Laundromat so that he could afford clean clothes.

He'd always heard that hard work was supposed to pay off, but all Bobby Ray could see in his future was more hard work and a constant, never-ending struggle. He supposed that's why he'd turned to betting. When one five-dollar bet on the dogs had made him more money than he earned in a month, he'd imagined himself a professional gambler. His lips twisted with bitter humor.

And that was exactly what Uncle Mackie had wanted him to think.

Within two weeks he was down two grand and panicking. Mackie's boys had roughed him up pretty good and had told him the next time they came back they wouldn't be so "gentle."

Bobby Ray had never been a saint and wouldn't pretend otherwise. He'd spent more time kicked out of all the various schools he attended than in them, mostly for fighting. Kids were smarter than people typically gave them credit for and they had a talent for sniffing out the kind that was different from them.

Bobby Ray had always been different.

For starters, his eyes were two different colors. Add the Glasgow smile—twin scars that ran from his ears to the corners of his mouth and made him look as if he was always wearing an unnaturally wide grin—compliments of one of his father's drunken rages, and he'd been an easy target. Life would have been a whole lot easier for him if he'd simply accepted the taunts and moved on, but Bobby Ray had never been able to do that.

He always fought. And he lost more often than he won.

Taking the first coin from Audwin Jefferson had been the most difficult thing Bobby Ray had ever done. Audwin hadn't stared at his scars or his mismatched eyes and hadn't cared if Bobby Ray hadn't graduated high school. He'd looked at him and saw an able-bodied man willing to work and the pride that had come with that knowledge had been damned near indescribable.

He bitterly wished he'd never known about the coins, wished Audwin had never taken the little black pouch out of the drawer and laughingly called it his retirement fund. He'd shown him a variety of different coins—buffalo nickels, Confederate money, various pennies and silver dollars, even a gold piece from Nazi Germany that his grandfather had brought back from WWII.

Sweating with dread and sick to his stomach, Bobby Ray had snatched the first coin his fingers had come in contact with and, feeling more miserable by the minute, had taken it to a pawn shop on the other side of town. The broker had given him a thousand dollars for the coin and Bobby Ray had promptly turned it over to Uncle Mackie, but by that point his debt had quadrupled.

And Uncle Mackie had found another way to earn a buck.

Because he'd become irrationally terrified of getting caught, Bobby Ray had started slipping the coins into the butter molds so that they were never actually on his body and then marking the molds with a small X so he knew where to find them. When he left the dairy to make the deliveries, he'd simply pull over and retrieve the coin, then head directly to the pawn shop and then to Uncle Mackie. Every time he thought he was close to paying off his debt, Mackie would fabricate another "fee" and get him on the hook again.

Because a couple of customers had complained that he was delayed, Bobby Ray had been forced to alter his system and start making his deliveries first. And that's when things had gone wrong. He'd set aside the mold he was certain held the coin, then belatedly discovered at the end of the day that it had somehow gotten swapped with a dud. By process of elimination he'd deduced that his coin had gone into Mariette's shop and he'd been desperately trying to retrieve it ever since.

She'd caught him last night and he'd panicked and picked up the dough roller. He hadn't meant to hit her with it—had only wanted to scare her away so that he could make a run for it—but she'd zigged when she should have zagged and it caught her on the back of the head.

She'd crumpled like a rag doll and he'd nearly been sick with fear. He'd dialed 911 from the shop phone, left the receiver on the kitchen counter and ran for it.

Because he needed to know how she was, Bobby Ray decided that he'd find a pay phone and start calling the local hospitals. The idea that he could have seriously wounded her—or worse—was eating him up inside. How had this happened? he wondered again, feeling the hopelessness close in around him. How had things gotten so completely out of his control? It was only a matter of time before Uncle Mackie turned up at the dairy, Bobby Ray thought.

And Audwin would fire him for sure then.

Dammit, he had to get that coin back. He *had* to.

"LISTEN, MARIETTE, I know that the guys have stomped in and taken over your protection and this case, but they mean well," Charlie told her once the afternoon crowd thinned a bit. "They consider you a friend. In their own weird way they genuinely believe that they're doing what's best for you."

"I know that," Mariette said, feeling trapped and exasperated. With herself more than anyone. "And it's not that I don't appreciate it because I do."

And that was true. She'd never had a father, or even a big brother for that matter, who'd had her back. It was odd having Payne insist on taking care of this problem because she'd always taken care of her own problems. Once she'd gotten over hearing so many orders fired at her regarding *her* house, *her* shop and *her* safety, she'd been able to stop and consider that and she'd found that, high-handedness aside, she rather liked that they wanted to protect her. That they thought enough of her to do that.

She'd just been so rattled this morning after the attack that she hadn't been able to think clearly. Mariette had never been afraid before, especially here in her own space. To find that she was vulnerable had been more than a bit disconcerting. She'd spent three hours in the E.R. and, despite various protests from all sides, had come back to the shop to start work. She'd had to—she wasn't just her own boss, she was also the boss of four employees and she did the bulk of the work.

If something got ruined or didn't turn out right, it had an immediate impact on her bottom line. She couldn't afford to just take off, not with dozens of pastries, cupcakes and cakes to make. Furthermore, if she'd gone upstairs and crawled into bed instead of continuing in her own routine… It felt too much like letting him win.

And that was simply unacceptable.

That said, despite the fact that she was equally dreading and anticipating Jack Martin taking over as her security guard tonight, Mariette had to admit that she was looking forward to being able to turn the watch over to him. She was dead on her feet and she could feel the hooks of exhaustion sinking in and tugging at her from all sides. She had a no-sleep headache on top of the headache the intruder had given her and would like nothing more than a warm cookie, a glass of milk and her bed.

With any luck, she'd be too tired by six o'clock to worry about lusting after Jack Martin.

Somehow, she doubted it.

Merely the thought of him made her nipples tingle and a heavy heat build low in her belly. She'd like to tell herself that the only reason she found him so irresistible was because she'd sworn off men for a while—sort of like the everything-looks-more-delicious-on-a-diet mentality—but she knew better.

Jack Martin was…different.

She'd felt it from the instant he'd walked into her

store. A quickening, an awareness of sorts, that had tripped some sort of internal trigger, made her more conscious of him. She was equally unnerved and transfixed. Not a recipe for contentment.

"This is my brother's first case for Ranger Security," Charlie remarked as she straightened a table-cloth. "Since coming out of the military." There was a strange undertone to her voice that Mariette couldn't readily identify. Sadness, maybe? Regret, definitely.

Intrigued, she turned to look at her. "Oh?"

Charlie bit her lip. "I know that we're not as close as you and Emma Payne are, and I really have no right to ask you this, but…" She hesitated, clearly torn.

"But what, Charlie?" Mariette wanted to know, genuinely curious.

"But could you take it easy on him, please?" she asked, her eyes softening with entreaty. "Don't make Jack pay for Payne's methods. My big brother has been through sheer hell the past six months and he needs to do this. He *needs* to help you. He needs to prove to them—and to himself—that he can."

Wow. Mariette didn't know what she'd expected Charlie to say, but that certainly wasn't anything she would have imagined. Jack had been through hell? What sort of hell? What did she mean by that? Her heart immediately swelled with compassion and a matching lump inexplicably formed in her throat.

She knew from Emma that Payne, Flanagan and McCann had all come out of the military after the death of a good friend and formed their security company. Was that the sort of hell Charlie was referring to? Had Jack lost someone? A friend? Had he been injured? Had he come out because he'd wanted to? Or because he hadn't had a choice?

Ultimately none of those questions were any of her business and yet she found herself desperately wanting to know the answers to them and so much more. It was hard to imagine a man as big and vital and alive as Jack Martin being anything other than formidable.

"His middle name is Oak," Charlie remarked thoughtfully. "Like the tree."

Mariette raised a brow. "That's different."

"It's a family name," she said. "I've always thought of him that way, too. Strong, rooted, weathering the storm, sheltering branches. When he came home he was…different. Not broken," she said quietly. "But definitely bent." She shook herself. "Sorry," she said, blushing slightly. She rolled her eyes. "He'd throttle me if he knew I'd said anything. I just worry."

"Of course you do," Mariette assured her. "He's your brother."

And she'd certainly given Mariette a lot to think about.

A splash of color from the storefront snagged her

attention and she turned in time to see a familiar round face smush against the window pane.

She smiled and nudged Charlie. "You want to see something that'll melt your heart?" she asked her.

Charlie nodded.

She gestured toward the door and then to Livvie. "Watch this."

"Dillon!" Livvie exclaimed, bouncing up and down on the balls of her feet, a smile wreathing her face. Dillon Melster, who also had Down syndrome, was Livvie's absolute favorite person in the entire world, which she would tell you in a heartbeat.

Wearing his traditional red baseball hat and his leather bracelet with the silver spikes, Dillon waved from the door, a big smile on his round face. "Livvie! Guess what?"

Livvie went up on tiptoe and leaned against the counter. "What?"

"I'm going to the 'quarium on Saturday to see the whales and Mom said you could come if you wanted to. Do you want to, Livvie? We'll get ice cream," he told her, as though getting ice cream was the most important part of the trip.

"In a waffle cone?"

"Sure. Or in a bowl."

"I like the waffle cone," Livvie told him. "It's more fun to lick. You can't lick a bowl."

Mariette smothered a grin. Livvie frequently

licked the bowls in the back when there was leftover icing. Evidently, she'd forgotten that.

Dillon's eyes widened and he beamed at her. "I've never thought of that before. You're so smart, Livvie."

Livvie blushed and ducked her head. "I got a new Hello Kitty necklace," she said, pointing proudly to the one around her neck. "See? It's got sparkles."

Dillon leaned forward so that he could get a better look. "Oooh, that's pretty. Where did you get it from?"

"Momma found it on the internet for me," Livvie told him.

Mariette leaned over to Charlie and whispered low. "Livvie's mother finds everything on the internet and if she doesn't find it there, then she hits up the Home Shopping Network or QVC. Her family should buy stock in FedEx," she said, laughing softly. "Try and recover a little of the money she spends."

Charlie grinned. "I can't say anything," she said. "I did almost all of my Christmas shopping online last year."

Mariette had bought a few things, as well, but still preferred being able to actually touch something before she bought it.

Charlie lifted her chin at Dillon and Livvie, a smile on her face. "They're adorable," she said. "They seem quite taken with one another."

She nodded. They were, and something about the pair warmed Mariette's heart. It was so pure, their affection. Uncomplicated.

She looked over and watched as Livvie showed him the newest picture of her cat, Piedmont. He was a fat orange-and-white tabby who, according to Livvie's mother, brought bird-watching to a whole new level and had the patience of a saint when it came to Livvie. She was forever trying to dress him up in her Hello Kitty finery. In this latest picture, she'd pressed a pair of pink heart-shaped sunglasses on his face.

"He's such a good kitty," she heard Livvie tell Dillon. "He sleeps at the end of my bed and keeps my feet warm."

"That's nice," Dillon said with a nod. "You see this?" he asked Livvie, pulling up his sleeve. "Bubba got me some ink."

Both Mariette and Charlie leaned forward so that they could get a look at the ink, as well. Mickey Mouse graced Dillon's forearm.

"Ink," she breathed, suitably impressed. "Do you think he could get me some ink?"

Dillon straightened a bit and grinned at her. "My brother can get anything, Livvie. For reals."

"I want a Hello Kitty ink," she said. "I'll put it on my arm just like you."

He beamed at her. "I knew you would like it. 'Cause you're cool like me."

She laughed delightedly and bounced on tiptoe again. "You want me to get you some tea? I'll put some cherries in there for you."

"Sure. Can I get a cookie, too? The kind with the candy bars in them?"

She nodded. "Yes, you can."

"Livvie, would you like to take your break now?" Mariette asked her and of course she said yes. She always took her break when Dillon came into the store.

Dillon's mom, who'd been talking on her cell phone, ended the call and walked over to the counter. She was a pretty forty-something divorcée who lived and breathed her children. Sadly, her husband hadn't shown the same devotion and had left shortly after Dillon's birth. She'd never remarried and had no plans to do so. For whatever reason, it saddened Mariette.

"The usual?" Mariette asked her.

She nodded and glanced over at Dillon and Livvie, a rueful smile sliding over her lips. "If it was up to him, we'd be here every day. He counts the minutes until he can see her again."

Mariette pulled a cranberry-orange muffin from the case and then poured her a cup of hot tea. She smiled. "He's a sweet boy."

"He is," she said, obviously proud. "And has more kindness and capacity to love than any man I've ever known. The world could learn a lot from my boy," she said.

Mariette watched as Dillon took one of the cherries out of his drink and popped it into Livvie's.

And she wholeheartedly agreed.

4

JEFFERSON'S DAIRY WAS A mom-and-pop organic farm that had lost the mom part six months ago. Audwin Jefferson was coping like many men who'd lost a wife—by throwing himself into the work.

The older gentleman was in need of a haircut and an iron, based on the wrinkled state of his clothes. The office garbage can was filled with cheap TV dinners and snack-cake wrappers, which Jack found particularly odd given the man's line of work. He believed in organic enough to make it and adhere to the strict government codes, but not enough to eat it himself?

He followed Jack's gaze and frowned. "Martha was the cook," he said. "I can fry an egg, but that's the extent of my culinary abilities and, now that I'm doing the books and the bulk of the work by myself, I don't have the time or energy to learn." He speared him with a direct look. "You married?"

Jack cleared his throat. "No, sir. I'm not."

He harrumphed. "Can you cook?"

"Not well," he admitted, feeling as though he were failing some sort of unspoken test.

"Well, if you're not going to marry—and so many of you young fools don't these days—then you'd best learn to cook."

His gaze drifted over a photograph that was sitting on his desk. Him and Martha, Jack imagined. Jefferson's hair was inky black, his shoulders wide and straight. Martha's hand was curled against his chest and she was tucked protectively under his arm. She'd been a beauty—a dark brunette with a great pair of legs.

"That picture was taken in nineteen sixty-four. I was twenty. Martha was seventeen. We were married forty-eight years," he said. His bushy brows tangled together in a frown. "It's funny the things you miss. Bacon frying in the morning. Panty hose hanging over the shower rod. The sound of her singing at the clothesline. She liked show tunes," he muttered, a fond smile on his lips. He looked up at Jack. "We weren't designed to be alone. Male and female," he said. "A matched set. And when you find the right one…" He drifted off. "Well, it's an indescribable happiness. I'm not saying it's all roses and sunshine—there has to be darkness to appreciate the light—but nothing is quite so wonderful as holding the hand of the woman you love."

For whatever reason, it was all Jack could do not to squirm in his seat. Hell, he felt as though he'd been called on the carpet and soundly chastised and yet he knew that wasn't at all what Mr. Jefferson had intended. He was merely mourning his wife and sharing it unashamedly with a stranger. There was honor in that, Jack knew, and had to respect it.

Mr. Jefferson blinked and then seemed to snap to himself. "Sorry," he said, mopping his face with a handkerchief. "Didn't mean to go off on a tangent. What can I help you with?"

Jack hesitated. Where to begin? "I know this is going to sound like a weird question, but have you had anyone steal butter from you recently?"

Jefferson's face went comically blank. "Steal butter?"

"Right," Jack told him, feeling more ridiculous by the minute. "One of your clients, Mariette Levine, has had thirty pounds of butter stolen from her over the past three days. The guy broke in again last night. When Mariette interrupted him, he threw a rolling pin at her and knocked her out cold."

Alarm raced across the older man's features and he leaned forward. "What? Is she all right?"

"She's fine," Jack assured him. "More annoyed than anything else, but we're checking every possible source to try and make some sort of connection. Since you're her supplier, I thought I'd check here first. See if you've had any similar occurrences."

"I haven't," Jefferson told him, a thoughtful expression on his lined face. "Business has run as usual." He frowned. "I just can't imagine why anyone would want to steal her butter. It doesn't make a damned bit of sense."

"Is there anything special or different about the butter that you supply Mariette?"

He shook his head. "Not a thing. I send the same thing to bakeries and restaurants all over the city."

"The packaging is the same, as well?"

"It is. Five-pound loaves."

A movement behind him snagged Jack's attention and he turned to find a young man with a pair of unfortunate scars on each side of his face peering around the doorframe. A blond, short-haired dog with large, alert ears and big brown eyes sat at his heels. "Sorry to interrupt, Mr. Jefferson." His gaze flitted to Jack and then away. "Just wanted to let you know that I was back."

Jefferson nodded and the boy turned to leave, clicking his tongue at the dog. "Come on, Prize. Time to get to work."

"Bobby Ray," Jefferson called, halting him. "Mariette Levine was attacked last night in her shop. Someone's been stealing her butter. Have you noticed anything odd? Seen anyone lurking about around here or her back door?" He looked to Jack. "Bobby Ray is my right-hand man and delivery guy. He's been an incredible help since I lost my Martha."

The younger boy blushed and ducked his head and instinctively reached to pet the dog, who'd nudged up under his hand. "Mariette was attacked?" he said, his voice cracking. He cleared his throat. "Is she all right?"

"She is," Jack told him, watching the kid carefully. He was awfully…twitchy.

"Have you noticed anything out of the ordinary, son?"

The boy thought about it for a minute, then shook his head. "No, sir. But I'm not looking, either. I make my deliveries and head to the next drop."

Jefferson nodded. "That's a good lad. Thanks," he said, dismissing him with a nod. The older man speared Jack with a direct look. "I don't know what's going on, but that boy doesn't have anything to do with it," he said. "He's a good kid that's been dealt a bad hand. Those scars on his face? His dad gave them to him when he was eight."

Jack winced, more than a little shocked. What sort of parent purposely disfigured their own child like that? And those were the scars that could be seen. God only knew about the ones you couldn't.

Jack nodded, accepting the warning for what it was, but didn't intend to completely dismiss the kid. Point of fact, he couldn't afford to dismiss anyone at this stage of the investigation. And while it was entirely possible that he was just the type who got nervous around an unfamiliar adult, he hadn't seemed surprised that Mariette had been hurt and that threw up a red flag.

Jack pushed to his feet and extended his hand. "Thanks so much for your time, Mr. Jefferson."

"Most welcome," he said. "Let me know if there's anything at all I can do."

"If you notice anything out of the ordinary or—"

"I'll call you," Jefferson told him. He winced. "I hate that for Mariette. She's a good girl with a good heart. And next to my Martha, she makes the best pound cake I've ever had. Tell her I'm thinking of her, will you?"

"Of course." Jack made the return trek to his car and noticed that Bobby Ray had retreated to his own car for a smoke break. The dog sat next to the back tire, seemingly guarding the boy. Was Bobby Ray nervous? Jack wondered. Or was this simply a regular occurrence? Either way, he bore watching. Jack made note of the tag and waved on his way out. As soon as he turned onto the main road he dialed the office and asked for Payne.

"What's up?"

"I need you to run a tag for me. I've got a first and middle name, but not a last."

"Sure."

"Bobby Ray. The car is an older model Buick." He reeled off the series of numbers and letters. "He's the delivery boy for Jefferson's Dairy."

"You think he's got something to do with this?"

"It's too early to tell," Jack said. "But he was as nervous as a whore in church when he walked in and found me talking to his boss."

"He could always be in some other sort of trouble."

That was true, Jack knew. Those scars, in addition to being a constant reminder of his father's abuse, had more than likely made him an easy target, as well. And kids could be so damned cruel.

"Jefferson warned me off of him. Said he'd been dealt a rough hand."

Payne whistled low.

"I see you've found him. His father did that. When he was eight."

"*Damn.* Poor kid. His name is Bobby Ray Bishop," he said. "He's nineteen. I'll run a full background check and forward it to you with his address."

"Thanks, Payne. I appreciate it."

"How's Mariette?"

"She's cooperating," Jack told him with less confidence than he actually felt, but when in doubt, bluff, right? "I'm heading back over there now."

Much as it galled him to admit it, he couldn't deny the twinge of trepidation tightening his gut. Him, afraid? Of a little slip of a girl? He'd waded into gunfire, fought his way out of countless battles when death had been a serious concern—and Mariette Levine and her dairy thief were making him nervous?

It was ridiculous, Jack told himself, tapping a thumb against the steering wheel. Utterly stupid. It was this case, his first for Ranger Security, his only in the private sector. That was the root of the problem. A fear of failure, of not knowing the proper rules, nothing more.

And if he managed to sell that line of B.S. to himself, then there was some beach-front property in Oklahoma he needed to look at, as well. Jack snorted.

Sexy woman + small space + overnight stay = hell on earth…squared.

And he knew it.

RESIGNED AND MORE THAN A BIT chastened for being less than grateful when Payne had first told her his security plan, Mariette had decided that she was going to do everything within reason to make Jack comfortable. And frankly, she was just vain enough to want him to, at the very least, like her. Probably that was stupid, but as evidenced by her most recent failed romance, she didn't always make the most intelligent decisions.

That was a thought she'd need to ponder later.

Additionally, whatever hell he'd been through that Charlie had alluded to—her heart gave an involuntary squeeze—would certainly be compounded by staying away from his own place, a fact she should have considered when she was mentally whining about her own inconvenience.

And this particular inconvenience was for *her* safety.

The very least she could do was be gracious about it.

At present Jack and Charlie were briefing each other and, in order to give them a bit of privacy, she'd retreated to her apartment above the shop. Because she spent so little actual time in this space she hadn't had to do much in the way of cleaning it up for company. She'd dressed the spare bed in clean sheets, stocked his bathroom with plenty of linens and had made sure that the batteries in the seldom-used remote control for the television still held a charge.

Because she was still putting the bulk of her disposable income back into the shop, her apartment had been decorated with hand-me-downs from her aunt, thrift-store finds, the occasional antique and do-it-yourself art.

She'd framed some of her favorite old album covers, picked up bits of old wrought iron and beaten-up architectural pieces salvaged from old homes. Her curtains were bits of scrap fabric with hot-glued hems and had been hung with pretty up-holstery tacks that she'd nailed directly into the window frame. It was junk-store chic, she liked to joke, but it was home and she loved it.

He rapped softly at the door and called her name. A line of gooseflesh raced down her back and she sank her teeth into her bottom lip as that same phenomenal need she'd experienced in the shop earlier broadsided her.

And she'd only heard his voice.

"In here," she said, feeling unaccountably nervous. *Geez Lord, Mariette. Get a grip.* She'd actually popped up earlier in the day and put a couple of baking potatoes into the Crock-Pot, an ingenious tip she'd learned from Aunt Marianne. Between her mother and her aunt, she'd been thoroughly educated on all things relevant and domestic. She felt a grin twitch at her lips. The whole how-to-choose-a-good-man lesson had been the only one that hadn't stuck.

Mariette had harvested enough fresh greens from her rooftop greenhouse—another little sanctuary—for a couple of salads and had just put the steaks beneath the broiler when she felt him move into the kitchen. The atmosphere seemed to change, become more charged. The fine hairs on the back of her neck prickled and a tremor raced along her fingers.

"Something smells good," he said, venturing farther into the room. His mere presence considerably lessened the space, made her feel small but, curiously, not claustrophobic. "I hope you didn't go to a lot of trouble."

Mariette smiled drolly. "Then you're different from the rest of your gender," she said, shooting him a look over her shoulder. "In my experience, men like it when women go to a lot of trouble, particularly where it pertains to food."

He chuckled softly. "A really good meal is a gift that most anyone with a brain should appreciate. Is there anything I can do to help?"

She gestured to two empty glasses on the counter. "You could put some ice in those. There's tea in the fridge."

Looking as at-home as it was possible to be for someone who didn't live there, Jack did as she asked. She darted another look over her shoulder at him, and smiled when she realized his head damned near brushed the suspended light fixture. She chuckled under her breath.

"What's funny?" he asked suspiciously. "Don't tell me I've done this wrong. I was always the official drink maker at our house growing up. Charlie set the table, I handled the drinks. I'm a champion tea pourer. I couldn't have possibly screwed this up."

Mariette laughed harder and shook her head. "It's not that," she said, giggling. "I was thinking about Livvie's 'corn man' comment earlier today." She turned the steaks. "Another inch and some green paint and you *could* pass for the Jolly Green Giant."

He sighed dramatically and shook his head. "Out of all the tall men she could have chosen, that's the one I brought to mind. A man in a leaf dress with girlie little booties on his feet?"

She swiveled to look at him. "He's wearing booties? Seriously?"

"This isn't the first time I've been mistaken for the big green guy," Jack told her. "It's always a kid's first frame of reference."

"And what tall man would you rather be mistaken for?" she asked, quirking a brow.

He shrugged magnanimously and took a sip of his tea. "Atlas works."

She felt a choked laugh break loose in her throat. "Atlas?"

"Hey, don't knock him," Jack told her. "It's a big job, holding up the world."

She turned back to the stove and chewed the inside of her cheek. "True," she conceded. "I suppose I'd rather be compared to Atlas than the Jolly Green Giant if I was tall, too."

"Damn straight," he said with a grim nod. "I'd never wear a dress or booties."

"But the loincloth would work for you?" Dammit, she shouldn't have asked that question because she could most assuredly see him being able to rock a loincloth. Her gaze turned inward at the thought and she unwittingly held her breath. *Sleek, sculpted muscle and fine bone structure, his masculine form a bare work of art...*

"I don't know about that," he said with a humble

nod. "But I'd prefer it to the other, that's for damned sure." He shot her a speculative glance and a wicked gleam entered his blue gaze. "I suppose you get mistaken for Julia Child all the time."

"Right," she said with a snort. "Because I'm also six two and we favor so much."

He arched a surprised brow. "Julia Child was six two?"

She nodded. Mariette Levine, gatherer of pointless trivia.

He hummed under his breath, seemingly filing that away. "You don't favor anybody I've ever seen," he said a beat later, his gaze drifting over her face as though trying to figure out what it was exactly that made her so different.

"Thank you," she murmured. Heat spread over her face. "I think."

"It's a compliment," he said. "You weren't at all what I was expecting."

Then that made two of them. Because she'd met most of the men who worked for Ranger Security she should have anticipated a fit, attractive guy—the rest of them certainly were. But none of them tripped her trigger the way this one had. She'd never looked at any one of them and felt her personal mercury hit critical mass in the time it took to draw a breath.

No man ever had, for that matter.

Remember the man hiatus, Mariette? Remember Nathaniel? Remember feeling stupid?

Evidently not.

"Oh?" she remarked, blatantly fishing. "How so?"

"I'd expected you to be older. I like your name—it's very different and it suits you—but it's a bit old-fashioned and, as such, I had this mental image of a plump, gray-haired granny with soft cheeks and laugh lines." He paused and sucked in a long breath, his eyes widening significantly as his gaze once again raked her from head to toe. "You're…not," he finished on a laughing exhale.

Wow.

"Not yet, anyway," she said, feeling feminine delight bloom in her chest and a corresponding tug deep in the heart of her sex. Mercy, that look…

And yes, she knew her name sounded old-fashioned…but that's not where it had come from. She inwardly grinned. Its origins were as unique and singular as her mother had been. And that was saying something.

She plated their steaks so that they could rest, then added the salad and potatoes and moved everything to the table. He pulled her chair out for her—an unexpected gesture she'd admit to enjoying—then took the seat opposite.

Mariette cleared her throat and cut into her baked potato. "My mother named me after her two favorite things," she said, her tone purposely light and matter-of-fact.

He carved off a bit of steak. "Really? What

was that?" He popped the bite into his mouth and groaned appreciatively.

Mariette dropped a large pat of butter into her steaming potato, then looked up and smiled. "My aunt Marianne and Smurfette."

5

JACK CHOKED, HIS EYES watering. He thumped his fist against his sternum and tried to swallow, then gulped down some tea.

Eyes twinkling, she continued to blithely eat her food. "You okay?" she asked, arching an innocent brow.

He cleared his aching throat. "Yes," he wheezed. "Just trying to make my lungs digest some food. Wonder of wonders, they're not designed for that."

She chuckled. "Sorry. I should have let you swallow it first."

"Smurfette?" he all but croaked. "Your mother named you after a little blue cartoon character? Seriously?"

"And my Aunt Marianne," she reminded him.

"That's...interesting," he said with a burst of air, because honestly he couldn't think of anything else to say. He'd heard lots of interesting names over the years and the tales of how they'd come about—hell, he was named after a damned tree—but this one… This one certainly took top billing for ingenuity and definitely fell into the WTF category.

"She had Down's," Mariette said, looking from beneath a sweep of dark lashes, evidently to gauge his reaction.

Oh. *Oh.*

Admittedly, this was a degree more shocking than how she'd gotten her name, but Jack kept his expression neutral. She'd said it without the smallest trace of self-consciousness or inflection. She might have said the sky was blue or "pass the salt." It was a simple, matter-of-fact statement. And it was in the past tense. Though he longed to ask several questions, he chose one he hoped was innocent enough.

He forked up a bite of salad. "What was her name?"

"Marlena."

"Also unusual," he commented, still trying to find footing in this treacherous terrain. "But lovely."

"She was a lovely person," Mariette said, her tone fond and wistful. "We lost her three years ago. Heart failure." She winced. "Sadly, it's all too common among those with the condition."

He swallowed. "I'm sorry."

"She was only seventeen when I was born," she said, continuing in that same flat tone. Her lips twisted into a bitter mockery of a smile. "My father, whom I fondly refer to as Wretched Bastard, was a caregiver at the day facility where she worked."

Oh, Jesus, Jack thought, reeling. He set his fork aside. That sick son of a bitch. Because she was his only point of reference, Livvie immediately sprung to mind and he wondered what sort of man it took to do something like that—something so heinous—to a person so innocent. So purely *good.* He set his jaw so hard he feared it would crack.

He closed his eyes, summoning patience from a higher source, then opened them again. "Please tell me he did time."

She snorted. "Not enough. Eighteen months."

Jack swore hotly.

She cocked her head, shot him a sad smile. "Everyone always assumes that having a mother with Down's had to be hard for me," she said, her gaze tangling with his. "But it was exactly the opposite. My mother was good and kind and loved me with the same sort of devotion any mother ever loved a child. She was the gentlest, sweetest person I've ever known." Her voice hardened. "Having that sort of evil for a father? Knowing that his tainted blood runs in my veins? *That* was the hard part."

He could certainly see where that would be true. Talk about two opposite ends of the spectrum. No wonder she was unlike any person he'd ever met. Her history was definitely more unique than anyone in his experience.

"Sorry," she said, giving her head a small shake. "I just find that it's easier to get that little bit of information out of the way. There are pictures of her—of us—all over the apartment and since you're going to be staying here…" She trailed off. "And it's not something I hide," she added, lifting her chin. "I was proud to be her daughter."

He completely understood. And he had no doubt that her mother was equally proud of her.

She straightened, her posture heralding a subject change. "So what did Mr. Jefferson have to say?"

Though he knew he'd have to review this conversation again at some point later, Jack laughed and wiped his mouth with his napkin. "You mean other than telling me to get married or learn to cook? Not a whole helluva lot actually."

Her pale gray eyes widened significantly and she laughed, the sound unreserved, full and throaty. Sexy. "Get m-married or l-learn to c-cook?" she repeated, still chuckling under her breath. "What did you do to provoke such a lecture?"

"What did *I* do?" he parroted, feigning offense. "*I* didn't do anything. I was merely looking at all the empty TV-dinner trays in his garbage can and that brought on the marriage sermon."

She winced, her gaze softening with sympathy. "Poor Audwin," she said. "I took a meal out there right after Martha died, but I haven't been back since." She paused thoughtfully. "I need to do that," she said. "If nothing else I can start sending a few home-cooked things with Bobby Ray when he brings my delivery by."

Ah. "Speaking of Bobby Ray," Jack said leadingly. "What do you think of him?"

Mariette paused to look at him and, much like Audwin Jefferson, something akin to irritation flashed in her gaze. She lifted her chin a fraction of an inch—he loved that quirk—and the mulish gesture was so reminiscent of his sister he wondered if Charlie had taught it to her already. "I think he's a sweet kid who's had a hardscrabble life and is constantly judged on his appearance rather than who he is underneath those scars." She nodded succinctly. "That's what I think of Bobby Ray. I am absolutely certain he has nothing to do with this."

All righty then. "Retract the claws, please, Mariette," Jack told her placatingly, essaying a grin. *Hey, underdogs, here's your champion*, he thought, admiring her spunk. "I'm not judging him on anything but the way he acted when I saw him at the dairy this afternoon."

She blinked, evidently falling off her soapbox. "How was he acting at the dairy? What do you mean?"

Jack hesitated, trying to pinpoint exactly what it was about the kid's behavior that had signaled a misgiving, set off an alarm. "He was bit squirrely," he said. "Unaccountably nervous."

"You're huge," she said, gesturing with a breezy hand to his body as though it should be obvious. "He was probably terrified of you."

Jack winced and passed a palm over his face to wipe away a smile. "You keep this up and I'm going to get a complex. Jolly Green Giant. Huge." His gaze tangled with hers. "I'm tall, Mariette," he explained with exaggerated patience. "The word you're looking for is *tall*."

Her eyes twinkled with unabashed humor and something else, something almost…sinful and damned sure dangerous. "Right," she said, nodding in concession. "No need to freak out. You're tall." She looked away, her eyes widening significantly, and chewed the corner of her mouth. "And a wee bit sensitive, evidently."

Jack laughed and shook his head. "Smart-ass."

She shrugged unrepentantly. "It's a gift," she quipped. She stood then and began clearing the table. "So, is that what you and Charlie were talking about then? Bobby Ray?"

Jack stood, as well, brought his plate into the kitchen, rinsed it off and loaded it into the dishwasher. She'd paused and was staring at him, seemingly transfixed.

"What?" he asked, perplexed at her expression. "Is there something on my face?"

"Are you married?"

That certainly came out of left field. Hadn't they covered this? In a roundabout way, at least? "No."

"Ever been married?"

"No."

"Then who trained you?"

He blinked. "Come again?"

"You just *got up from the table, rinsed your plate and loaded it into the dishwasher.* That's *learned* behavior. It's not normal to your kind."

He laughed out loud, the sound a bit rusty from disuse. Clearly it had been too long since he'd really laughed. "My kind? What am I? Some sort of foreign species?"

She shot him a speculative glance, one that seemed to peer directly into his brain, and grinned. "I don't know what you are, but you aren't normal, that's for sure."

Well, if lazy assholes who didn't appreciate a meal well enough to help clean up was her normal then he was glad, in this instance, to be *ab*normal. Of course, this line of thought brought on a completely new set of questions, ones he didn't have any right to ask. If he was the exception to the rule, then who had been the guy—or guys, he thought ominously—who'd made it? Who'd been the lazy, ungrateful dickhead who'd set the damned precedent?

He instantly hated him, whoever he was.

Irrational? Most definitely. He cast a brooding glance at Mariette, who was busy dumping the leftover salad into a plastic container. The overhead light cast a golden glow over her dark hair, picking up the rich auburn tones. He loved her hair. It was long and hung in wavy layers that framed her face and curled ever so slightly around her beautiful, full breasts.

Longing knifed through him, cutting him to the quick. Heat raced through his blood and settled in his groin and his fingers itched with the need to touch her, to see if her skin was as soft as it looked. Particularly the smooth line of it that ran over her jaw. He caught her particular scent, something slightly exotic with vanilla undertones.

She wore a long-sleeve, lime-green shirt with her logo emblazoned on the pocket and a pair of jeans that were worn and comfortable looking. They didn't so much hug her frame as caress it, molding around her curves as though they'd been especially designed with her in mind. She'd kicked off her shoes—he'd noticed them by the door when he'd come in—and was padding around in her socked feet.

There was something especially endearing about that, but for the life of him he couldn't have explained why. They were feet, for heaven's sake. And the socks were cute, inasmuch as he imagined socks could be. Hers were white with little black Scottie dogs scattered all over them. The dogs were wearing red bowties.

She paused and her gaze followed his. She wiggled her toes and grinned. "Don't make fun," she said. "Livvie gave them to me."

He leaned a hip against the countertop. "I wasn't going to make fun. I like them."

Her smile widened. "I'll tell her so that she can get you a pair, as well. You never answered my question."

"What question? There's been a question amid all the insults you've hurled in my direction?" he teased.

She ducked her head. "Showing me your sensitive side again, are you?"

Jack took a deep breath. "Honest to God, woman, you—"

Her gaze slid away from his, but he caught the curl of her lips all the same. "I'd asked you if that's what you and Charlie had been talking about," she interrupted. "Bobby Ray?" she prodded.

Oh. Right. "As a matter of fact, yes," he said, reminded of his real purpose here. Flirting, fun as it was proving to be, wasn't it, dammit. "I know that you think that he's not involved in this, but I still believe he bears a little investigation."

Skepticism wrinkled her otherwise smooth brow. "Based on him being 'nervous'?"

"Physical tells are just as significant as verbal ones."

She momentarily stilled, then looked over at him. "What do you mean?"

How odd. If he didn't know any better he'd think

she was the nervous one. But what the hell could she possibly have to hide?

"I mean that sometimes our actions give us away long before our mouths do." His gaze dropped to hers and he had to force it back up. *Exactly like that*, he wanted to say.

She licked her lips and swallowed. More torture. "He could have been nervous for a variety of reasons, couldn't he? Did you talk to anyone else at the dairy? Anyone besides Audwin?"

"No," he admitted. "But I've got a background check running on Bobby Ray and am going to do the same thing with the rest of Mr. Jefferson's employees. If there's a red flag, then I'll find it."

"But not Audwin?" she asked, a smile playing over her lips. "What makes you so certain that it wasn't him who threw the dough roller at me?"

Jack crossed his arms over his chest and studied her for a moment, then came to an interesting conclusion. She was arguing for the simple sport of it. How bizarre that he found that attractive, when he couldn't remember ever liking this sort of conversation before. Of course, he wasn't used to a woman arguing with him. No brag, just fact. They typically agreed with everything he said and fell right into bed with him. He'd always liked that—it was expedient, uncomplicated—but wasn't so sure he would now. She'd…changed things.

Damn.

"You said your attacker was tall and skinny," he told her, determined to prove his point, if for no other reason than to show her that he could. "Audwin is not. He's on the short side with a potbelly, and I'd be willing to bet if I looked in his closet he wouldn't have a sweatshirt much less a hoodie." He shot her a grin. "I am certain, however, that I would find lots of flannel. Furthermore, Audwin is left-handed and based on the way you described what happened, your guy threw with his right hand. Additionally, Audwin's hands are so riddled with arthritis I doubt he could grasp a rolling pin well enough to pick it up, much less throw it at you with any accuracy whatsoever." He pulled a shrug. "Based on those things I was able to rule him out as our possible offender."

She blinked owlishly at him for a moment, evidently absorbing that information. "And you got all of that from what little I said and one meeting with Audwin?"

He nodded. "I did."

She looked insultingly surprised. "Well, I guess you know what you're doing, then."

A dry bark of laughter erupted from his throat before he could stop it. Talk about damning with faint praise. He'd been a friggin' Ranger, dammit. One of the best trained soldiers on the planet. "One would hope."

She had the grace to blush. "I'm sorry," she said. "That didn't come out exactly the way I'd intended.

I'm sure you know what you're doing. It's just that there's really not that much to go on. Payne can't leave you here indefinitely and—"

Jack chuckled and shook his head. "Do you know Brian Payne?"

She frowned. "Well, of course I know him. I've known him for years. He—"

"Then you know that once he's taken something on he's not going to let it go until it's finished." He leveled a look at her. "I'm afraid you're stuck with me until then."

Her eyes rounded and she muttered a curse. "It's not that. I don't mind that you're here, really."

He just stared at her.

"I don't!" she insisted. "I don't like being told what to do and that's how this whole thing was presented—after I'd been knocked unconscious, by the way, so I wasn't really at my best—but I honestly don't mind and I'm genuinely grateful that I have friends who want to protect me." She swallowed. "It means a lot."

A woman who didn't like being told what to do? How novel, Jack thought with a snort. And he supposed having her home and place of business seemingly hijacked after another asshole had broken in and assaulted her would make her feel a bit out of control. He couldn't fault her for that.

He smiled and released a deep breath. "It means a lot to me, as well. This is my first case and if I can't catch a damned Butter Bandit, then I'm in the wrong line of work."

She lifted her shoulders in a weak shrug and grinned wanly. "He's slippery."

"He's an amateur who has gotten lucky," Jack told her, laughing at the bad pun. "I also think he's someone who is familiar with your setup here, otherwise he wouldn't know exactly what he was doing."

She winced. "I'd actually thought about that." She pursed her lips. "I still don't think it's Bobby Ray."

Interestingly enough, she didn't sound nearly as convinced as she had before. He hated to destroy her illusions about the boy, but there was something not right there. Call it a gut instinct, a premonition, a second sense or whatever, but every bit of intuition he possessed told him that the boy was involved somehow.

And Mariette wasn't the only one who was going to be hurt if Bobby Ray was ultimately behind this— Audwin Jefferson would be, as well. The older man had been just as quick—if not quicker—to jump to Bobby Ray's defense.

And if both of them were willing to stick up for him, then they had to see something in him that compelled that sort of response. Audwin seemed like a decent enough judge of character and, no longer than he'd known Mariette, he could tell she wasn't the sort of person who wasted her regard on those who didn't deserve it.

There was much more to this than what met the eye, Jack decided. He just hoped he was able to find out what that was before any more damage was done.

Mariette hid a yawn behind her hand.

"You must be exhausted," Jack told her. "You couldn't have gotten much sleep last night."

"Not of the restful sort, no," she admitted. "I keep early hours. I'm normally in the bakery by 4:00 a.m."

"Four?" Damn. That was early.

"I have a two-day policy," Mariette told him. "If something sits in the case for more than forty-eight hours it goes to various agencies around the city—I don't throw them out. I can't abide the waste. But I like to keep the front stocked with my freshest products. That means all new stuff every other day."

He nodded, impressed. "It seems to be working for you."

"It is," she confirmed, a rather pleased tilt to her ripe little mouth. "But I work hard, so that's only fair, right?"

"Most definitely." His gaze drifted over her face, noting the fatigue weighting her lids. "Why don't you go on to bed, then? I'll keep watch."

"All night?" she asked, evidently alarmed. "But when are you supposed to sleep?"

"I'll sleep," he told her. "I've got to set some alarms for the doors and windows and I'm going to review some stuff that Payne was supposed to forward to me. I'll catnap," he assured her, touched by her concern. He was used to his mother and sister fussing over him, but this was a new experience. Pleasant as it was, he wasn't altogether sure he liked it. "I'm used to long hours."

And he fully expected the ones that loomed in front of him to be some of the longest he'd ever experienced.

The hottest, most interesting woman he'd ever met sleeping in a bed mere feet from him—and she had to be off-limits.

Nothing more than self-preservation told him that.

6

DESPITE THE FACT THAT she was beyond exhausted, Mariette couldn't sleep. Typically, this wasn't a problem. Because she wasn't the sort of person who could leap out of bed and be happy and alert and ready to conquer the day—rah! rah! rah!—she was up at three, coffee in hand by three oh five. She liked to check her email, update the website for the shop and ease gently into her morning, like slipping into a warm bath.

By the time she'd had breakfast, showered and tidied up her apartment she was grounded enough in her own company to be able to face the day. From the moment she went downstairs until after 6:00 p.m., she didn't get a single minute to herself unless it was to go to the bathroom.

And she was open seven days a week. The church crowd always came by on Sunday mornings and, until she got the bulk of her equipment paid for and her mortgage paid off, she didn't anticipate being able to change her hours or take a full day off. She did close at one on Sundays, but ordinarily used that time to try new recipes and perfect others, and if she wasn't doing that, then she was hosting birthday parties, baby showers or bridal teas.

In short, she was always busy—there was always something to do—and, as such, being able to fall asleep was never a problem. Drifting off on the couch on the rare nights she tried to watch a movie or read a book was a more common issue. Maybe that was part of her Problem With Men. Impaired judgment from lack of rest? Mariette gave a mental shrug. In lieu of anything else, she'd take it.

Nathaniel, aka Crooked Dick, had been forever insisting that she take off and leave one of her girls in charge and, while she imagined that seemed like a reasonable request, Mariette had just never been able to do it. She'd put everything she had into her business—building it had to come first. She should have known when he'd made the you-make-cookies-you're-not-saving-the-world comment that he wasn't the guy for her.

Asshole.

She didn't give a damn if she was a Porta-Potty cleaner, she'd still give it her best effort. *Anything worth doing is worth doing right*, Aunt Marianne used to always say.

Interestingly enough, she got the impression that

Jack Martin was the same, adhered to the same standard no matter what he was doing. He seemed just as concerned with catching her Butter Bandit as he did with anything else. No doubt those especially keen observation skills and attention to detail had made him a fine soldier.

Honestly, it was those very skills that had made her unaccountably nervous. If he'd seen that much after a few minutes interviewing Audwin Jefferson and a passing glance at Bobby Ray, then what had he noticed about her? What sort of observations had he made?

She was almost afraid to speculate.

Mariette had never mastered the art of hiding her feelings. If she was mad, she said so. If she was happy, she said that, too. Living with her mother, she'd had to be an excellent communicator and therefore never tried to hold anything back or hide. While her mother might have missed sarcasm and the like, she was top-notch at reading moods, could pick up on the tiniest shift in Mariette's demeanor. Even if she'd been so inclined, there'd been no point in trying to conceal her feelings.

And until all six and half feet of his splendidly proportioned frame had come walking through her door she'd never had to worry about it.

But no one had ever affected her quite so strongly before in her life. No one had ever made her feel *so much*. On a physical level, he didn't just flip every switch, he fried the circuits. *The size of his hands, the breadth of his shoulders. All that mouth-watering muscle.* The hot way he ducked his head and smiled when imparting a small joke, the simple quirk of his lips, the barest hint of a dimple in his cheek…and she became a quivering, all-but-drooling pile of goo.

She released a shaky breath.

And then there was the way he moved. It was one of the sexiest things she believed she'd ever seen. It was this loose-hipped, rolling sort of gait that telegraphed his strength, his confidence, his very badass-ness. There was something uniquely intense about him, a banked sort of energy bubbling just beneath the surface. Still waters might run deep, but Jack Martin was more like a tsunami.

And seeing that kind of power gentle with a smile for a girl like Livvie. Seeing the genuine tenderness in his gaze, his desire to please her…

Now, that was some kind of man. That took strength.

And he was in her living room, Mariette thought, her nipples tingling at the thought. She could hear the low hum of the television, the occasional noise that signaled a shift on the couch, a clink of ice hitting the side of a glass. For whatever reason, she'd imagined having a man stay here with her would feel odd, would pollute her space, even—despite her poor choices, she'd never let a man sleep over before—but Jack seemed to be the exception to that rule.

When she'd come out to tell him good-night after taking her shower, she'd found him staring at a photograph on her mantel, a soft smile on his lips. It was one of her favorites—a candid Aunt Marianne had taken of her and her mother at the beach. She'd been five at the time. They'd had on matching sun hats, sitting toe-to-toe, legs spread-eagle, building a sand castle between them. They'd worn the same identical expression of concentration.

"You were a chubby kid," he'd said, pointing out a fat roll, then had gestured to the painted flames canvas in the hearth where a real fire would have been if the chimney would have worked. "Toasty."

Mariette giggled, remembering, and flopped restlessly onto her back. Glanced at the clock. Three minutes had passed since the last time she'd looked at it. Sheesh. This was ridiculous. He was here so that she *could* go to sleep, so that she could rest without worrying.

How ironic that her very protection would be the thing that would keep her up at night.

She was too tightly wound, too aware of her own body and it had been too long since her last orgasm. And he was too hot and too close and too…everything else.

A low throb built in her sex in time with the steady beat of her heart and her nipples pearled even tighter behind her pajama top. A soft hiss slipped between her lips and she shifted, pressing her legs more tightly together to ease the seemingly unending ache.

If anything, that made it worse.

Mariette rolled her head to look at the clock again and then whimpered softly in frustration. Two minutes since the last time. Shit. She was doomed. There was no way in hell she was going to be able to fall asleep in this sort of state. With a resigned sigh, she pushed up out of bed, slipped her feet into her Betty Boop house shoes and padded quietly into the living room.

Jack smiled when he saw her and pulled one of those small earbuds from his left ear. He'd been looking at something on his laptop screen, but nonchalantly closed the lid when she'd walked in.

Too nonchalantly.

Damn, she hoped he hadn't been watching internet porn. Watching porn while he was supposed to be protecting her would demote him from perfect-guy status and kill her lady-bits-quiver-for-him permanently.

"Is something wrong?" he asked, his brow wrinkling. "Am I keeping you up?"

In a manner of speaking, yes, but she could hardly say that, now, could she? He'd changed into a pair of loose pajama pants, the kind that tied at the waist, and a dark T-shirt. His gun was lying within reach on the end table and seeing it gave her a little shiver of dread. She sincerely hoped he wouldn't need that.

"No," she lied. "I was just thirsty." She pointed awkwardly to the kitchen and, feeling ridiculous, headed in that direction.

Liquor, Mariette thought. Liquor never failed to put her to sleep. She'd never been much of a drinker—preferred to have control of herself at all times—but on the rare occasions she'd indulged she'd ended up quite mellow and sleepy. She poked around in the cabinets, trying not to make too much noise in the process, and then finally located the bourbon she typically used to make praline sauce. Rather than dirty a glass, she just ducked low and tipped the bottle up.

It belatedly occurred to her that she probably looked like an alcoholic sneaking a quick fix, which was of course the moment Jack cleared his throat.

"How rude," he chided from the doorway, an amused smile on his lips. He tsked. "You could have at least offered to share."

Curled up in the backseat of his car, which he'd parked at a local truck stop, Billy Ray huddled deeper into his coat and tried in vain to keep his teeth from chattering. He'd stayed inside the diner for as long as he could without drawing any suspicion—or getting run off for loitering—then had reluctantly left the cozy warmth for his chilly Buick. He couldn't afford to run the car all night—it would use too much gas—and wished he would have thought to bring a blanket from his motel room.

He was absolutely freezing.

But at least he was alive.

And if Uncle Mackie got ahold of him, he knew he'd be praying for death, so, ultimately, this was the better alternative.

Because he knew Uncle Mackie had someone watching his motel room, he didn't dare go back there—wasn't safe—and now that the big guy was snooping around for Mariette, he couldn't afford to attempt to go after the coin again.

At least not yet.

He'd have to at some point—he wouldn't have a choice—but doing it on the heels of what had happened last night would no doubt be a terrible mistake and he'd made so many of those already...

At least he hadn't seriously injured her, Bobby Ray told himself, still appalled that he'd hit her with that damned dough roller. He liked Mariette. She didn't look at him the way other people did, with suspicion in their eyes and a predisposed inclination to distrust him.

Like Audwin, Mariette never failed to offer him a real smile—he knew the difference, was familiar enough with the other kind to spot the genuine article—and usually insisted that he take some sort of snack with him when he left her shop. He'd cruised by after he'd left work and, to his profound relief, had spotted her in her usual place behind the counter.

Despair closed in on him again and he could feel tears clog the back of his throat. He swallowed them back, forcing them to recede. Bad things always happened when he cried. In fact, he hadn't shed a tear since he was eight years old and his old man had given him this ghastly permanent smile.

He always found it odd that people stared at him—he couldn't bear to look at himself.

He really hated that he'd mucked things up, that he'd made such terrible decisions, that, ultimately, he was stealing from the only people who'd ever made him feel like more than a second-class citizen, but he just didn't see any other way. He either paid Uncle Mackie back or they'd hurt him and Billy Ray was sick to death of being hurt. Of being someone else's punching bag.

If he could only get the coin…

What was it one of his foster mother had always said? *If dreams were horses, then beggars would ride.* He laughed miserably.

That pretty much summed up the state of things, didn't it?

It was hopeless, Bobby Ray thought. There was no way out. And until he got that coin back he had no choice but to take another one.

The mere idea made him sick and his stomach suddenly heaved. He quickly leaned over and emptied it into the floorboard, then wiped a shaky hand over the back of his mouth and fought misery.

As usual, he lost.

JACK FOUND MARIETTE crouched furtively in front of the kitchen counter, bottle tipped back like a seasoned drinker. He enjoyed the blinking, miserable alarm that skittered across her expression the minute he'd caught her.

Eyes wide, her long dark hair hanging in a tangled curtain around her face, she slowly lowered the bottle and winced at the burn. "This is not what it looks like," she said in a low wheeze.

He raised a brow and leaned against the doorjamb. "Oh?"

Rather than get up, she exhaled mightily, settled on her rear end and relaxed against the cabinets. She wore a pair of pale blue flannel pajamas decorated with cupcakes and a to-hell-with-it resigned smile. She lifted her shoulders in a small shrug. "It helps me sleep."

"They make medication for that, you know."

She took another swig, the delicate muscles in her creamy throat working as she swallowed and then hiccupped rather adorably. "This is faster."

He chuckled and shook his head, sincerely hoping that it wasn't his fault that she couldn't sleep. He didn't think that he'd made that much noise, but who knew? He'd actually turned up the volume on his hearing aid so that he wouldn't miss any noise from downstairs and had been watching one of his lip-reading tutorials online to pass some of the time.

He had to do something that was going to require enough of his attention to forget about her being just a room away.

As the night progressed, he'd become more aware of her and less concerned with the consequences.

Not good.

Honestly, when she'd walked into the living room after her shower, her face scrubbed clean, her nose shiny and all that hair pulled up into a wet knot on top of her head… Just remembering made blood race to his groin, made his balls tighten and his dick swell. Unbound breasts, the hint of nipple behind fabric, that generous ass…

Hands down one of the sexiest things he'd ever seen.

And, remarkably, she'd been fully clothed.

At least, on the surface, anyway.

He imagined that the rest of her skin beneath the fluffy floor-length chenille robe she'd been wearing was just as lovely and dewy soft as her face had been. He didn't know what sort of soap she'd used—though he fully intended to investigate that later out of nothing but sheer curiosity—but it had followed her into the living room and had smelled so damned good he'd wanted to slide his nose along her neck and inhale the skin in the hollow of her collarbone. It was something exotic with vanilla undertones, sexy and wholesome and unaccountably mouthwatering.

She was mouthwatering.

And knowing that she was so close—all but breathing the same air—and yet untouchable had been unbelievably torturous. He'd desperately needed a distraction, one that would require a great deal of concentration on his part, so watching the videos had been his first thought.

And they were typically his last, as well.

Jack had come to terms with leaving the military, had even been able to shift the blame off his shoulders because, ultimately, he'd done everything he was supposed to do. War was war and there were times when, even with every precaution in place, people were still going to get hurt, still going to die. Seeing any life cut short was awful—heart wrenching—but he'd had a soft spot for Johnson. The boy had been barely twenty, smart and hardworking with a moral compass that didn't drift the way so many of his contemporaries did. The military had made a man out of him much more quickly than the real world would have done and he'd acclimated well, with grace and wisdom beyond his years. He'd had so much potential and his death, aside from being horrible, was such a waste.

That he'd been desperately trying to share his dying words with Jack—his expression, the fear, the very need that had been written in his panicked eyes—was something that haunted him mercilessly. He could remember *everything* about that encounter down to the last detail, from the specks and smudges of dirt on Johnson's face to the way his mouth moved while he was talking. It wasn't until he went to get his last hearing aid and he'd noticed a teenager at the clinic lip-reading that it occurred to him that he could learn, and once he learned it, he could figure out exactly what it was that Johnson had been trying to tell him.

Once that was done, he could finally close that chapter of his life and move on. Or as much as he imagined he'd ever be able to, anyway. But if it had been important enough that he'd spent his last breath trying to share it with him, Jack knew that this was something that he couldn't simply ignore. He had a duty to the boy to see whatever it was through.

And he would.

His gaze drifted over Mariette once more, her lush little body hugged in warm flannel, her creamy cheeks pinkened from the alcohol and a pang of longing—and something else, something much more significant and harder to define—shot through him. He'd never met anyone quite like her before, who engaged every single part of him the way she did. The desire was legendary, singular even, and more pressing than anything he'd ever experienced…but it was much more than that.

She was much more than that.

She was intriguing, a mystery, an enigma wrapped in cupcake pajamas and vanilla scent. She was hardworking and tenderhearted, creative and smart, loyal to those who earned her favor and quick to champion them if she felt they were threatened.

She was also single, which boggled the mind.

He couldn't believe that no one had snapped her up yet. That some enterprising young professional hadn't dragged her to the altar and impregnated her posthaste. Because he was unnaturally curious about her, Jack had looked at every picture that was on display and noted the distinct absence of a current or even a past significant other. He couldn't imagine that it was anything but her choice. So...why? Had the actions of her father so permanently put her off men that she'd paint them all with the same brush? Or was it something else?

These were things that were none of his business and yet he fully intended to find out the answers to them.

Irrationally, he *needed* to know.

She looked up at him, her pale gray eyes a little less focused than they were previously, and with a slow smile of the mildly impaired, offered him the bottle.

Chuckling under his breath, Jack sidled forward and accepted it, then placed it carefully on the counter. He offered her a hand. "Think you can sleep now?"

She looked at his hand as though it were a foreign object, then back at him, almost balefully. She swallowed hard. "Probably not, but I should try."

With a resigned sigh she grabbed hold and allowed him to help her up. She stood a little too quickly, wobbled, and fell against his chest. She inhaled sharply at the contact—a telling breath, both music and doom to his ears—and looked up at him.

The need he saw there nearly felled him.

She was soft and warm, her unbound breasts pressed against him and her scent tangled around him. He was literally burning up from the inside out and yet he was frozen, couldn't have moved if his life depended on it.

He'd instinctively wrapped an arm around her waist to keep her from falling and, though he knew he should let go, couldn't seem to get his brain to make the required command that would move her away from him, that would disconnect whatever it was that was happening between them. This close he could see little bursts of green radiating from her pupil and a tiny freckle to the bottom left of her eye.

He was hit with the insane urge to taste it.

Need slammed into him, gluing his feet even more firmly to the floor, and his heart decided to abandon traditional beating and move at a skipping, breakneck pace that made him light-headed and breathless. *Him,* breathless? He swallowed a maniacal laugh as he considered the incongruity. This sensation, this phenomenon, was so intense and so singular he didn't know whether to be thrilled or terrified.

Her wide-eyed gaze was strangely confused and resigned as it searched his, then darkened and dropped hungrily to his mouth.

He went hard.

She noticed.

She released a fatalistic breath, muttered "Oh, to hell with it," and then went up on tiptoe and pressed her mouth to his.

The shock of it—the sheer perfection—made him stagger against the counter and he pulled her with him. The road to hell might be paved with good intentions, Jack thought, but the heaven along the journey was bound to make up for the eventual destination.

Surely they wouldn't fire him over a kiss—just *kissing* their friend, Jack thought dimly, and if they did…

Screw them. It was worth it.

7

HAD SHE NEVER TOUCHED HIM—had he never offered
her that beautifully large, masculine-veined hand—
Mariette imagined that she might not have behaved
so shamelessly. She might not have stumbled into
his magnificently muscled frame and, had she never
known what it felt like to be held so closely by someone who a) turned her lady business into a sauna,
b) made her feel strangely protected and safe and c)
had the most kissable mouth she'd ever seen, then
she might have been able to summon the required
wherewithal to back away from him.

She was supposed to be practicing The Hiatus
From Men, after all.

But since Jack Martin did that and oh-so-much
more, she'd been doomed to failure.

Depending on how one decided to look at it.

And considering she was too busy trying to see

if she could crawl out of her skin and into his, she wasn't looking at anything at all.

She was relishing the deliberate, wholly thrilling slide of his lips against hers, the taste of his expert tongue as it plunged into her mouth and swept the sensitive recesses with a skilled sort of accuracy that most men never bothered to learn because they were too busy trying to move on to the next base.

Despite the fact that she could feel his *more than substantial* erection nudging high up on her belly and she knew that he was as reluctantly snarled up into this mindless heat between them, Jack had made no impatient move to take things to the next level.

He was feeding at her mouth as though that was all that mattered, as though kissing her fulfilled some sort of precious, deeply seated need. He was allowing this first kiss to be just that—a first kiss. The most anticipated and romanticized milestone for couples throughout time and throughout the world. A first kiss could either doom a budding relationship or make it bloom into something special, but ultimately, a lot rode on that initial contact.

In addition, a woman could tell a lot about a man by the way he kissed. If he was sloppy, drippy or in a hurry, then you could bet that he hadn't worked on his other techniques. A good kisser—a man who knew when to suckle, when to slide and when to slip (and, oh, did Jack ever)—was usually one who'd paid enough heed to the little things to ensure that he was going to give the same sort of thorough attention to every other part of the sexual process.

No doubt Jack Martin was a phenomenal lover.

The mere thought made her entire body quicken with anticipation, made the fine hairs on her arms stand up, her sex slicken with moisture and throb. Her bare breasts felt too heavy behind her shirt, too sensitive and too neglected. Mariette pressed herself more firmly against him, slipped one hand along his jaw, savoring the line of bone and soft skin, then pushed the other hand into his hair and let the silky strands tangle through her fingers.

He tasted like minty toothpaste and sweet tea and his particular scent—something musky and crisp—wrapped around her. He was hot and hard, more physically attractive than any man she'd ever met, and with every purposeful slip of his tongue into her mouth, the more fully she settled into the deep, open vee between his legs. The countertop had to be digging into the small of his back, but if he noticed or cared he never made an objection.

He left off her mouth and slid his nose along her jaw, breathing her in. "Hmmm," he murmured. "I've been thinking about doing that all day."

A shiver ran down her spine and gooseflesh peppered her too-hot skin. He framed her face with his hands, kissed the underside of her cheek. It was tender and sensual and something about it triggered a peculiar feeling in her chest.

It jarred her enough to make her pull away, albeit reluctantly.

She couldn't afford to make another wrong decision and something told her there wouldn't be any coming back from Jack Martin. He'd ruin her heart if he broke it.

She peered up at him and smiled self-consciously. "I think I'd better try to get some sleep now."

He grinned. "That would probably be a good idea."

She didn't move, but looked away, released a sigh and shook her head. "You know I'm not going to be able to look you in the eye in the morning, right?"

"I hope that isn't the case," he said. "You've got the prettiest eyes I've ever seen."

Startled at the compliment, she turned back and her gaze collided with his. Though throwing herself at his mouth and practically scaling his perfect body hadn't made her so much as bat a lash, the simple remark made her blush clear to her hairline. "Thank you," she managed, because it seemed like the right response.

He inclined his head. "Welcome."

Feeling uncharacteristically shaken and unsure, Mariette turned and started to make her way back to her room.

"Mariette?"

She stilled, darting him a look over her shoulder. His golden hair gleamed in the semidarkened room and a rueful smile turned the impossibly sexy lips she'd just been kissing. Atlas, indeed.

"If it makes you feel any better, I would have made the move if you hadn't. The only reason you beat me to the punch was because I was too damned stunned by how much I want you, to react. Even knowing that you're a friend of my new employers and they'd kick my newly hired ass—" though, admittedly, it would take all three of them "—wasn't enough to keep me away from you." He leveled a look at her. "If you'd like to request another agent, then now's the time to do it."

He didn't have to add "Or else you know where this is going to lead," because she knew it. She knew that if he stayed here the ultimate conclusion to this hellish attraction would involve the two of them and a bed…and probably the shower and the wall and the kitchen table, as well.

Those visions obligingly took root in her fertile imagination and the image of his gloriously naked body looming over hers, that sinfully carnal mouth suckling her breast sent a barb of heat directly into her clit, making her resist the urge to squirm.

He pushed off from the counter, grabbed the liquor bottle and took a long pull. "Just let me know what you want to do in the morning and I'll take care of it," he said. "And I'll own it."

Meaning, he'd take the blame and wouldn't leave an iota of it at her doorstep.

He was definitely a different sort of man, Mariette thought. The sort that was going to get her into trouble, no doubt.

But when had that ever stopped her?

JACK WATCHED MARIETTE turn and make her way to her room. He waited, until he was certain she was out of earshot and not going to come back, to swear theatrically but quietly under his breath.

He'd known, hadn't he? He'd known the instant he clapped eyes on her this morning that she was going to prove to be more temptation than he was accustomed to resisting. And now that he'd tasted her, felt that lush, womanly little body bellied up to his? The only way to keep this from reaching its ultimate conclusion was by taking himself out of the equation.

Was he proud of this? Not especially.

Jack had never met the irresistible woman…until now.

He'd had friends' girlfriends and wives hit on him over the years, couldn't go into a bar without a girl making some sort of pass at him. He didn't have to beat the women off with the proverbial stick, but he didn't have to do much to attract them, either. He guessed he was passably handsome, tall and fit, had all of his teeth, didn't live with his mother and was gainfully employed.

All of that certainly put him working ahead of the curve.

But this fatalistic, all-consuming, out-of-his-mind *need* that he felt for Mariette Levine was out of the realm of his experience. It was uncharted territory and he was navigating without a map.

He supposed he could try to lie to himself and insist that he could keep things on a strictly superficial level, but despite the fact that he'd been told he could sell ice to an Inuit, Jack knew better than to try and sell himself this self-righteous, self-serving load of B.S.

He'd known before he'd kissed her that she was going to set him off and now that she had? You couldn't put the bullet back in the gun.

It was *done*.

That's why he was giving her the choice, why he'd given her an out.

It was gallingly pathetic how much he hoped she didn't take it.

Ordinarily he'd be worried that fraternizing with a client would end up getting him fired, but since Charlie and Jay had met on the job—and so had most of the other Ranger Security agents, the three founding members included—he didn't see where he could possibly be kept to a standard none of the rest of them had managed to keep. He didn't imagine that they would necessarily like it—Mariette was a friend, after all—but they weren't hypocrites.

They could hardly fire him over something they'd all done, right?

Right.

If she'd just stayed in that room, he thought, trying to get a handle on himself. But no, she couldn't sleep. Perversely, he wondered how well she was sleeping now. He imagined it couldn't be any better than it was before and almost wished it was worse.

He'd been miserable before, thinking about her being in that room, close but not close enough. Now he was in agony. Because he'd touched her, tasted her, felt her hot little body pressed to his, the reciprocated desire in her kiss, the greedy way she'd slid her hands all over his body.

She wanted him every bit as much as he wanted her. That, at least, was gratifying.

His cell suddenly vibrated at his waist and he checked the display. *Charlie.* He rolled his eyes. Perfect timing, as always.

"Yeah," he answered by way of greeting.

"Bobby Ray lives at a pay-by-the-week motel out on Dearborn," she said.

He frowned. There hadn't been a current address in the file Payne had sent over, only the one of his last foster family who had said they hadn't seen or heard from Bobby Ray in more than a year. "How did you find that out?"

"I used my special skills."

He grinned and chewed the inside of his cheek. "Who did you hack this time?"

"That's for me to gloat about and you to never know," she quipped. "Anyway, I waited for a couple of hours for Bobby Ray to show up and when he didn't I went in and talked to the night manager."

"Was he helpful?"

"He had some interesting information to share, yes. He said that Bobby Ray hadn't been back to his room for the past three days, but that a couple of people had been by looking for him."

Ah. He could only imagine what kind of people. "Did the manager know who they were?"

"No," she said. "I suspect he's lying about that, but short of vaulting across the counter and putting him in a choke hold until he told me the truth, there was nothing I could do about it."

He was genuinely surprised that she hadn't. He chuckled. "What stopped you?"

A beat slid to three and she swore low under her breath.

Jack frowned. "Charlie?"

"I haven't even told Jay yet," she said. "Dammit, I can't believe I just did that."

Told Jay what? Did what? Jack felt his eyes widen and he drew a quick breath. "Oh, my God. Are you—" He knew they'd been trying, but...

"Yes," she said, sounding equally exasperated and overjoyed. "And if you breathe a word of it before I—"

"I won't," he assured her, smiling wonderingly. A bizarre sensation winged through his rapidly expanding chest and he gave his head a little shake, trying to wrap his mind around his sister—his scrappy little *badass* sister—becoming a mother. He swallowed, his eyes inexplicably darting toward Mariette's room. "You'll be a wonderful mother," he told her. "Congratulations, little sister."

"Thank you. You're going to make a great uncle," she said fondly.

Evidently done with the mushy stuff, Charlie cleared her throat, all business once again. "All right, back to Bobby Ray. I think you should spend some time watching his motel tomorrow and see if they come back. The night manager says Bobby Ray's rent is up day after tomorrow and that if he's not there to pay up for another week, he forfeits whatever he has in there. Considering that all he has in this world will fit in that little dingy room, he probably wants it."

He imagined she was right.

"Whoever these guys are have frightened him enough to keep him from coming back. That makes him desperate. And desperate people often act in ways they ordinarily wouldn't."

Another Bobby Ray convert, Jack thought. But he understood. He'd read the kid's files, the ones he was able to get through the legitimate channels and the ones that had required Charlie's specialized skill. His foster care file was three inches thick and read like a horror novel. The permanent record she'd managed to pull from the last school he'd attended hadn't been any better. In fact, both documents had painted a picture of a kid who had never been given a modicum of affection, much less a break.

He'd known about his father giving the boy the scars—he hadn't known that his father had done the same thing to his mother "so that the two would match" and that her cuts had been too deep and had resulted in her death.

"I found something else that was interesting, too," Charlie told him.

His senses went on point. "What was that?"

"I let myself into his room and—"

"You what?" he asked, his voice rising. "Have you lost your damned—"

"Hush," she interrupted. "I found a receipt for a headstone in the bedside drawer," she told him. "It was dated a month ago and was twenty-three hundred dollars."

Damn. Where in the hell had the kid gotten that kind of money? A lottery ticket? He doubted it. Otherwise, why were those men following him? And he certainly wouldn't have made that at the dairy.

"It was for his mother," Charlie confirmed sadly. "There was also a printout from the local hospital. Judging by the leftover pain killers and bandages, Bobby Ray ran into some trouble a few days after he bought the memorial."

Jack frowned. Whatever the boy had gotten into, he was definitely in over his head. No wonder he'd been nervous when Jack had shown up at the dairy. He was probably terrified that he'd been part of the crew who was clearly chasing him.

"I'll watch the place tomorrow," Jack told her. "And I'll go by the hospital and see if I can find out anything about Bobby Ray's visit."

"They're not going to tell you anything," she said. "Confidentiality laws. And their computer systems are much more complicated than you'd—"

Jack merely smiled. "You've got your methods, I've got mine. You let me handle it."

"Whatever," she said in that patronizing you're-wasting-your-time tone of hers.

"And Charlie?"

"Yes?"

He braced himself, because he knew she wasn't going to like what he had to tell her. "You stay away from that motel."

He could feel the blast of her anger before she said a word. "Look here, Jack. I am perfectly capable of taking care of—"

"Stay away," he repeated. "Or I'll have a chat with your husband. And your bosses."

She called him something their mother would certainly object to and then disconnected.

A lead at last, Jack thought.

And he knew beyond a shadow of a doubt it was going to royally piss off and disappoint both Mariette and Audwin.

Unfortunately, it couldn't be helped. And he had a job to do.

The next morning Jack found a Post-it note stuck to his bedroom door. It was a single word note and hadn't been signed.

Stay.

8

MARIETTE WASN'T ALTOGETHER certain what was up with Charlie, but she was pale and sullen and not at all the otherwise happy, chatty person she'd been the day before. Because she could be paranoid with the best of them, Mariette wondered if she'd somehow managed to inadvertently telegraph the fact that she'd been crawling all over Charlie's brother the night before and, possessing just as keen observation skills as her brother, she'd noticed it.

Mariette released a sigh. "Charlie, have I done something wrong?"

Charlie looked up at her and blinked. "What?" She grimaced. "No, no," she said, shaking her head. "I'm sorry. I'm just in a funk this morning." Her lips twisted with a wry smile. "When I was trying to persuade Payne, Jamie and Guy into bringing Jack on board after the accident, I was so busy thinking about how wonderful it would be to have him home

and work with him that I'd forgotten what a pain in
the ass he can be."

While all of that was very interesting, the thing
that intrigued her the most was "after the accident"
comment. She winced sympathetically, even though
she had no frame of reference for Charlie's predica-
ment.

She was an only child, after all, though she'd
always imagined that having a brother or sister
would have been nice. She'd had to make do with
imaginary friends. She'd had one named Charmin,
she remembered, and in her imagination, Charmin
had borne a remarkable resemblance to Casper the
ghost.

"What accident?" she asked as blithely as possible, considering her level of curiosity.

Charlie muttered a curse, squeezed her eyes shut
and then bumped the back of her head against the
wall as though to knock a little sense into it. "I am
losing my freaking mind."

Well, hell. Mariette wiped down another table.
"It's fine," she said. "Sorry I asked."

"No, I'm the one who's sorry," she said, seemingly at a loss. "I keep slipping up. I've never been
really good at keeping secrets, but lately I've been a
lot worse."

"If it's a secret, you don't have to tell me. Really,"
she insisted. Naturally, she was dying to know. No
doubt because it pertained directly to Jack and any

nugget of insight—any key to figuring out what made him tick—was of interest to her.

Charlie cast a furtive glance out the front window, then looked back at Mariette. "It was an IED," she confided in low tones. "He was lucky, ultimately. Two of the men who were with him were not." She winced, her face softening with regret. "One of the boys was only twenty and Jack had talked about him often, seemed to really like him. The boy—Johnson, he called him—lost both of his legs. He bled out and died in Jack's arms."

Mariette's stomach rolled, her heart gave a squeeze and she covered her mouth with her hand. "Oh, no."

"I know," Charlie told her. "I don't know how you move past something like that. How you cope after seeing something so horrible happen to a friend. To anyone, really," she added.

Mariette either, for that matter. Justice was one thing—punishment for a crime, particularly those against children, she could handle. Senseless death was another matter altogether.

And what of Jack and his injuries? Mariette wondered. Granted he looked absolutely perfect to her, but how was it that he was able to walk away from a blast like that without any visible scars? Not that she'd seen all of him yet, but…

The key word there being *yet,* Lord help her.

"Jack's eardrum was shattered so badly that it

took three separate surgeries to repair it," Charlie said, answering her unspoken question. "He wears a hearing aid in his right ear," she said gesturing to her own and Mariette couldn't have been any more surprised. She hadn't noticed it at all.

Charlie's lips quirked in sadness. "That's why he's grown his hair out," she told her. "So that it covers it up." She shook her head. "And it's not vanity. It's the idea that someone might think he's compromised or incapable. You have to understand, Mariette, my brother was our hometown golden boy. All the girls wanted to be *with* him and the guys wanted to be *like* him. He was the star quarterback, the valedictorian of his class, the conquering hero every time he came home." She released a low breath. "Except this last time. People treated him differently, as though he were damaged and no longer deserving of the pedestal they'd put him on. It was heartbreaking to watch, more difficult than anything I would have ever imagined." She glanced up. "Do you know what a soldier hates more than anything?"

Mariette's mind had been quickly processing Charlie's words into images and the resulting pictures were heartbreaking. She blinked, belatedly returning her attention to Charlie.

"No," she said, shaken. "What?"

Charlie's shrug was melancholy. "Being pitied. He gladly made his sacrifice and would do it again and give more. And the people who pity him are the ones who don't get that. That's what's difficult to move past." She sobered, cast another glance out the window. "You can't let on that you know," she said. "He'd throttle me."

Mariette swallowed, nodded her promise. "I won't."

"Had you noticed the hearing aid?" she asked.

"No, I hadn't." And she was relatively certain she'd been breathing quite heavily into that ear at one point last night. She felt a blush stain her cheeks and watched Charlie's eyes sharpen with interest.

"He'd be pleased about that. I hope he's been a good guest," she remarked. "Not using all your hot water or leaving dirty dishes in the sink. That was always a pet peeve of our mother's. Dishes went into the dishwasher, period."

"He's fine," she said, because really what could she say? *Your brother makes me hot and last night I came dangerously close to riding him like a mechanical bull at the fair on my kitchen floor? And, oh, yes, he did put his plate in the dishwasher?*

Er…she didn't think so.

As for tonight, she didn't know what was going to happen, though she had her hopeful suspicions, of course. But when he'd offered to have himself removed from this case and someone else assigned in his place, Mariette had known a blind sense of panic that was completely disproportionate to the occasion. She'd known the instant he made the offer that she was going to refuse, but had been too shocked by her own reaction to address it right then.

Because refusing meant admitting that she wanted him as much as he said he wanted her. It meant she was going blindly into another relationship when she knew better. When she knew that she needed to stop for a while and take stock of what she genuinely wanted out of a man so that she wasn't constantly putting her hopes into the wrong one.

And as much as the idea of telling him not to go terrified her, letting him leave without seeing what this was between them was more frightening.

There was something about him that she knew was different. Better. Wishful thinking? Possibly, because who wanted to be wrong again? But she didn't think so. Jack Martin held a special sort of appeal, a spark that marked him as a true original. Mariette sighed.

Clearly the insane attraction had left her mentally compromised. There could be no other explanation for her utterly shameless, wanton behavior. She blinked, struck with sudden insight. He'd turned her into a tramp, Mariette realized. Was it horrible that she rather liked that?

The bell over the door tinkled, signaling a new customer. "I hope that smile is because you're happy to see me," an amused male voice said.

Mariette's grin capsized and her gaze slid reluctantly to the speaker. "Sorry to disappoint you, but no." She glanced at Charlie. "Would you mind helping him? I have something I need to see to in the back."

Looking equally baffled and intrigued, Charlie nodded and stood. "Of course."

Nathaniel sighed and a muscle flexed in his suddenly tight jaw, making a liar of his smile. "I was hoping to talk to you, Mariette," he said. "You can't give me five minutes?"

She turned and glared at him. "No."

He darted a look at Charlie, then back at Mariette and took a step forward. "Really, Mariette," he hissed. "This has gone on long enough. You know how I feel about you and I know how you feel about me."

She was going to send him the bill when she ground all the enamel off her teeth. "If you knew how I felt about you, Nathaniel, you wouldn't bother coming in here anymore. It is over." She smirked at him. "Say hello to Tiffany for me."

He rolled his eyes. "Oh, for heaven's sake, Mariette, that meant nothing. You know that," he insisted.

"And that's supposed to make it *better?*" she asked, dangerously close to losing her temper. "It's done. Move on," she said, wearying of this conversation. "I have."

His bravado slipped. "What do you mean by that? Moved on how? With who?"

"Would you like a cupcake?" Charlie interrupted cheerfully. "Perhaps a cookie or a croissant?"

He flicked his gaze to her, then located Mariette once again. "This is ridiculous, Mariette. I'll be by at six when you close up and we can talk about this then."

Perhaps Nathanial was the one who needed a hearing aid, Mariette thought. "No, we won't," she said. "You are not welcome here anymore."

Infuriatingly, he shot her an indulgent grin. "We both know you don't mean that. See you at six." And before she could utter another single word, he strolled back out onto the sidewalk.

Charlie's eyes were wide and her mouth hung open in apparent shock. "What the hell was that all about?"

Mariette sighed. "That's my ex," she said. "But, as I'm sure you've noticed, he doesn't seem able to grasp the 'ex' part."

"Perhaps someone should help him," Charlie said, her voice throbbing with anger. "What a self-important, condescending, arrogant little ass. Who's Tiffany?"

Mariette chuckled at Charlie's apt description of her ex. She'd thought some of those same adjectives applied the first time she'd met him, but then he'd just kept asking her out and she let her vanity mistakenly revise her opinion. "The girl I caught gargling his balls the last time I went to see him at his office," she said, her lips curving into a bitterly droll smile.

Charlie's eyes widened. "Damn."

"It was never going to work," Mariette told her. "I was more broken up over my poor judgment than anything else." She shook her head, genuinely baffled. "What in the hell was I thinking?"

"I'll admit I was just wondering that myself," Charlie told her.

Mariette chuckled. "I can't say as I blame you."

"You should mention this to Jack," she said with a succinct nod. "He'd get rid of him for you."

She'd just bet he would. "I can handle him."

"Yes, but why would you when you don't have to?"

"I'll think about it," Mariette said. She'd admit that it would be quite gratifying to see Nathaniel's smug smile vanish at the sight of Jack. No doubt he could do some serious damage to those pricey veneers. She glanced at Charlie. "Have you heard from Jack today?"

"Earlier," she said. "He called to gloat."

This sibling rivalry/affection was quite fascinating. "Oh?"

"He was able to procure some information that I didn't think he'd be able to get." She snorted and rolled her eyes. "He's impossible when he's right."

"Congratulations," Mariette said with an eyeroll of her own. "You've just described the male species."

Charlie chuckled and her gaze turned soft. "They have their redeeming qualities," she said. "Mine actually saved my life. I had no choice but to marry him."

Stunned, Mariette goggled at her. "He saved your life?"

She nodded. "He did. He charged into a burning house, found me and carried me out." Her gaze seemed to turn inward, remembering. "He nearly died trying to save me."

"Wow." Inexplicable envy twisted through her. It must be something to be loved like that. To have someone so determined to protect you that they'd offer themselves up instead. That their own life became insignificant. Her mother would have done that. Even her aunt, Mariette would admit. But she'd never had anyone who wasn't blood related love her like that.

And *that's* what she wanted, Mariette thought with a dawning sense of comprehension. She wanted what Charlie had. That's why she kept trying, kept giving guys who didn't deserve it the benefit of the doubt.

Was she happy with her life? Yes. She had a business she loved and a home of her own. She was proud of her accomplishments. But wanting to be loved—truly, genuinely loved—was something she imagined every person wanted. While other people might think that made her weak, Mariette knew better.

Because at least she was strong enough to admit it.

Charlie laughed softly. "Wow, indeed," she said. "Try trying to win an argument with that sort of ammunition." She rolled her eyes. "I-saved-your-life pretty much trumps everything else."

Mariette imagined so.

Charlie sighed, seemingly wrapped up in her own thoughts. "Jack is actually going to be back a little early today. I've got an errand to run."

Mariette nodded, envious of her new friend. "Thanks for being here, Charlie," she said. "I'm truly grateful. I know that you've probably got more exciting things that you could be doing than babysitting me all day."

"Not at all. I—" She suddenly clasped a hand over her mouth and darted for the bathroom with a garbled "Excuse me."

Five minutes later, her face pale and her hands a little unsteady, she made her way back into the dining room. "I'm sorry. I must have eaten something that didn't agree with me."

"From here?" Mariette asked, alarmed. She was fanatic about expiration dates and making sure that everything was fresh and clean. She immediately started scanning the contents of her display cases, suspicious of everything in there now. She hoped that—

"No, no," Charlie quickly assured her. "Nothing from here."

She'd seen Charlie eating a macaroon earlier. She hoped like hell nothing was amiss with those. Several dozen of those had gone out for a baby shower this morning. The last thing she wanted to do was make the expectant mother and all her friends sick. *Damn.* A note of panic made her belly flip.

"Do you think it was the macaroon?" Mariette asked her, her worried gaze swinging to Charlie's. "I didn't see you eat anything else. Did you eat anything else? I—"

Charlie put a hand on her arm. "Mariette, I promise you nothing from your case has made me ill." Her lips rolled into a smile. "Seriously. You don't have to worry."

Charlie almost looked amused, which, frankly, annoyed the hell out of Mariette. This was her business, her livelihood. "It's just I sent a large order of those out—"

"I'm pregnant," she blurted out. "It's morning sickness, not your macaroons." Her eyes rounded in immediate dismay. "Shit, shit, shit," Charlie lamented, evidently regretting the impulsive outburst. "That's twice now, dammit, and I haven't even told Jay yet." She looked up at her. "See?" she said. "This is what I mean. I'm just spewing it out there—" she gave an airy wave of her hand "—and can't seem to help myself."

Dumbstruck, Mariette felt a grin slide over her lips and her gaze inexplicably dropped to Charlie's still-flat abdomen. "That's because it's harder to keep good news a secret."

A light suddenly gleamed in Charlie's gaze. "You know, you're exactly right."

"You should tell Jay," she said. "Before you tell the mail man or your dry cleaner or a total stranger."

"I know," she said. "But I wanted to make it special. Plan a romantic dinner or something and I haven't come up with anything that's over-the-top spectacular."

Mariette grinned. "The *news* is what's over-the-top spectacular, you little nitwit. How you tell him isn't important—it's the telling him that is." Mariette glanced at her case, then back to Charlie. "But I do have an idea if you're interested in hearing it."

"Of course."

"See those chocolate eggs in the case?"

Charlie gasped and nodded.

"Initially I only made them for Easter, but they were such a hit with the kids I stock them year round. Those have a creamy filling, but I could give you a hollow one and you could—"

"Yes!" Charlie interrupted delighted. "Yes, yes,

yes!" She gave Mariette an impulsive hug. "How quickly can you put it together?"

"I've got some hollow eggs in the back," Mariette told her, pleased that she could help. "You give me what you want put in it and I can have it ready in a couple of minutes."

"I've got the perfect thing," Charlie told her. "I'll call Jay and have him come down." She hugged her again. "Oh, thank you, Mariette. You're brilliant. An egg," she said wonderingly, her eyes gleaming with happiness. "How fitting."

"I'll warn you now," Mariette told her. "I'm going to hide behind the counter so that I can watch his reaction."

Charlie grinned and she practically bounced on the balls of her feet. "I don't care if you hang from the ceiling à la *Mission: Impossible,*" she said. "I just can't wait to tell him."

And now neither could she, Mariette thought, smiling, happy to be a part of it. Thrilled though she was, a twinge of unexplainable melancholy pinged her heart. She'd have to think about that later, Mariette thought, annoyed with herself.

These Martin siblings were seriously messing with her head…and possibly with her heart, as well.

9

Bingo, Jack thought as he watched the two thugs climb out of the older-model navy blue Cadillac. He knew enough about goons to spot one and both of these guys had more brawn than brains. And knowing what he knew now after visiting the hospital, it took every bit of restraint Jack had not to spring out of the car and pummel the living hell out of both of them. Damned bullies. He *hated* bullies.

Unfortunately, until he knew exactly what he was dealing with, he suspected he could make Bobby Ray's situation worse rather than better. His best plan of action at the moment, much as it galled him and went against the grain, was to gather information and find out who they were.

Then pummel the hell out of them.

Harsh? Not in his opinion. After what the pair did to Bobby Ray, they needed the ever-loving hell beaten out of them and he grimly suspected Bobby

Ray had never had a single person ever mete out any justice—or even mercy, for that matter—on his behalf.

But Jack would.

Looking first left and then right, they strolled up to Bobby Ray's door and knocked. They didn't look as though they expected a response, but were merely following orders. The two shared a look and the taller of the two shook his head. They turned then and made their way to the office. They were inside and back out in less than a minute, presumably because the attendant on duty didn't have anything more to tell them than the last time they were here.

Jack snapped a couple of pictures with his cell phone and noted the tag number so that he could find out exactly who they were. Once they were safely out of the parking lot, he went in to pay the attendant a visit, as well.

The kid behind the counter was in goth dress with black eyeliner, black lipstick and unnaturally black hair. Parts of her face were pierced in places he'd never seen and he imagined would be intensely painful.

"Those guys who were just in here," Jack said, jerking his head toward the door. "Do you know who they are?"

She picked up a bottle of black—surprise, surprise—nail polish and shook the bottle. "Don't have a clue," she said, managing to sound massively dis-interested with those four words.

"Have you seen them before?"

She slid the brush over her thumbnail, but didn't bother to look up. "A few times."

Damn, he'd lost a word. This was going nowhere fast. "Were they looking for Bobby Ray?"

"Yep."

Down to one. He exhaled mightily. "Have they left a number or asked for a call if Bobby Ray shows up?"

"Nope."

That was interesting. If his rent was up soon then, like Jack, they had to realize that the boy was going to try and come back for his stuff.

"Those men want to hurt Bobby Ray," he said, taking a gamble that this girl was merely feign-ing disinterest. Her hand had trembled across the second nail and she'd spread paint over the edge of her finger. "They beat the hell out of him with a bar of soap shoved down into a sock about a month ago."

The poor kid. Once he'd explained who he was and why he was interested in knowing exactly what had happened to the boy, the nurse he'd confided in at the hospital had pulled the file, opened it to the correct page and then conveniently left to go see about another patient.

By the time she'd returned, Jack had been gone, but the information he'd seen there had been enough to make him sick to his stomach. A Good Samaritan had brought him in. His back and abdomen had been covered with bruises, the deep-tissue kind that were intensely painful and long to heal. Contrary to popular belief, a sock beating *would* leave bruises and it hurt like a bitch.

A reaction at last. She looked up. "It was them? They're the ones who did that to Bobby Ray?"

Hmm. He took another chance. "Were you the one that took him to the hospital?"

She swallowed, seemingly unsure.

"I don't want to hurt him," he said, hoping she believed the sincerity in his voice. "I want to help him. I don't know what he's gotten himself into, but he clearly isn't able to get out of it alone."

And Jack did want to help him. Regardless of whether or not the boy had anything to do with what was happening to Mariette, he still wanted to figure out what was happening with Bobby Ray and try to make it right.

For whatever reason, because there certainly was no physical resemblance, Bobby Ray reminded him of Johnson. Different boys, different backgrounds, but there was a similar kind of core, an essence of something good. Given the kid's history, Bobby Ray should have been in prison by now. But he wasn't. He was working, supporting himself. Trying. Against all odds and virtually any hope, as far as Jack could see.

That took courage.

And as far as Jack could tell, the first people to ever pay the kid a kindness were Audwin and Mariette—he'd never had anyone who had his back.

Furthermore, if he was involved—and Jack still believed that to be the case—then he suspected Charlie was right, that he was desperate.

The girl was thoughtful, stared at him, more than likely trying to decide if she trusted him or not. "They're coming back tonight," she finally said. "They're going to rent the room next to his."

And wait him out. Shit.

And he'd come back, Jack knew. He'd have to. Everything he owned was in that little room. A precious little by the world's standards, but it was all Bobby Ray had. Obviously, Jack would need to see about protecting it.

So the first order of business was to get the kid's stuff out and eliminate his need to return. "Can you let me into his room? I'll pack up his stuff and make sure that he gets it."

She was shaking her head before he even finished. "Look, I realize that you're probably the lesser of two evils, but I can't just give you access to his room and let you take his things."

"Then I'll pay you to do it," he said. "The most important thing is to keep him from coming back here. They're going to jump him if he does." He paused. "I suspect the first beating was a warning.

This one…" He purposely left the sentence unfinished so that she could complete the thought herself. "You can figure out a way to get it to him after all of this is resolved," he said. "Meet up with him somewhere else, a place of your own choosing."

She nodded. "I'll do that. But you don't have to pay me. I like Bobby Ray." Her direct gaze was a bit unnerving. "He looks beyond the surface of things. Sees what's on the inside and judges that for himself. You'll let him know I've got his stuff?"

Jack nodded, thinking that looking beyond the surface was a lesson everyone—himself included—could stand to learn. "I'll get word to him and tell him to call you. They don't appear to know where he works," Jack told her. "If you do, then keep it to yourself."

She nodded.

"Do you know why they're looking for him?" he asked.

Once again, she hesitated. "I have my suspicions," she said.

He waited, letting her make up her mind.

"I don't know who they are, but I know who they work for," she finally told him. "A guy everyone calls Uncle Mackie. He's a bookie." Her lips twisted bitterly. "And once you're on his hook, you're never off it."

Jack had pretty much worked that out for himself. He'd ruled out any kind of drug-related trouble because, despite being terrified, the kid's eyes had been clear. Furthermore, Audwin wouldn't have tolerated it. Audwin trusted him with the truck, after all, and if the old man suspected the boy was using there was no way in hell he'd let him drive.

He nodded, made sure to look her in the eye. "Thank you."

"Don't let anything happen to him," she told him. "He's a good guy."

Jack thought so, too, but one who'd let a bad decision take him down a road that could get him seriously hurt and put the ones he cared about in equally serious jeopardy.

Hopefully he could prevent that.

"Bobby Ray, you've got a visitor," Audwin called, poking his dark gray head around the door.

Bobby Ray felt his knees weaken and his stomach roll. Oh, God. They'd found him. He didn't know how, but they had. His mouth went bone-dry. "Who—Who is it?" he asked, terrified to the bone.

"It's Jack Martin, that friend of Mariette's. Said he needs to talk to you."

Not any better, really, Bobby Ray thought miserably. But he didn't think he'd try to hurt him here, anyway. It would look odd if he refused to see him, so he couldn't do that. Feeling only slightly less nauseous, Bobby Ray wiped his sweaty face with the back of sleeve—he'd had to turn his shirt inside out to hide the dirt—and made his way to the front. He found Jack Martin with a booted foot propped up against the fence, looking at some cows. He'd chosen a spot a bit away from the office, Bobby Ray noted, and couldn't decide if that was a good thing or a bad thing.

He twisted the brim of his hat nervously in his hands. "You wanted to see me?"

Jack Martin turned, his eyes assessing. "Those thugs who are chasing you and roughed you up last month are renting the room next to yours tonight and they're not going to leave until you show up."

Shit. Bobby Ray didn't know what was worse— that this man knew his business or having Uncle Mackie's men parked next door to his room, preventing him from returning so that he could get his things. He didn't have much, really, but there were some pictures of his mother that he couldn't bear to part with and a few of himself before the scars. He liked to look at those. To imagine how life might have been different if he'd never gotten them. Though he had plenty of memories before the scars, he'd taken them for granted, had taken being normal—looking normal—for granted, as well. People either stared as if he was an exhibit in a freak show, or wouldn't hold his gaze. It was awful.

"Geneva is collecting your things and getting them out before they return," he continued. "She said for you to call her and she'd meet you some-where."

Still reeling, Bobby Ray nodded. "All right." Geez God, how did he know all of this? Why had he both-ered to find out? And what had he said to Geneva to get her to help him? Geneva was more distrustful of people than he was, and that was saying something. He liked her. She was kind and had pretty eyes.

"I work for Ranger Security," Jack told him, an-swering the bulk of his questions with that one ad-mission. "I'm providing security for Mariette until the break-ins at her shop are resolved. We have an agent covering her during the day and I'm there at night. All night," he added, shooting him a look. He heaved a sigh. "Look, Bobby Ray, I know that you're somehow connected to this. I don't know how, though I think I have a good idea why, but I know it all the same. Whatever it is that you've gotten your-self into, I can help you get out of it."

Bobby Ray snorted before he could stop himself. Yeah, right. All he was trying to do was trick him into confessing and he'd be in cuffs so quick his head would spin. And once he was behind bars there would be no getting out. He didn't have money for bail, no one to call. Once Audwin knew he'd taken some of his coins, he'd lose his job and the old man's respect. He'd be disappointed and angry. And Mari-ette... She'd never forgive him for hitting her.

And why should she, really? It's not as if he deserved her forgiveness. He should probably just give up, Bobby Ray thought. Stop running and let them do their worst. It was only a matter of time before everything blew up, until the whole damned thing came to light.

He'd almost rather be dead.

"You've got people who care about you, Bobby Ray. Whatever it is that you've done, it can't be unforgivable."

If only that were true, Bobby Ray thought. And he genuinely wished he could believe it. That he could confide what he'd done, why he'd done it and figure out a way to make amends. But that would not resolve the Uncle Mackie issue and his so-called debt would continue to build. He'd never be free of him.

"How much are you into Uncle Mackie for?"

Bobby Ray looked sharply at him and at the look, Jack Martin merely smiled. "Here's my theory," Jack told him. "I think your first bet made you believe that you'd hit a lucky streak and you thought you'd found a way to make some quick, easy cash." He gestured toward the farm. "This is honorable work, but it's hard and the pay can't be that great because of Audwin's overhead."

Bobby Ray swallowed.

"You weren't so lucky with your next bet, or the next and, ultimately, by the time you knew what had happened, you were in way over your head and Uncle Mackie had you right where he wanted you—

into him and afraid. See, I know Mackie's game," Jack remarked. "Bookies like making easy money, too, and if they can charge exorbitant interest and fees on unpaid debt and then scare you into finding a way—*any way*—to pay it back, then they've got a golden goose, a veritable endless ATM machine. *You,*" he said significantly. "It's my suspicion that you've taken something from Audwin and he hasn't figured it out yet. And whatever you've taken, you've hidden in one of the butter loaves. But you lost track of one—the one you needed—and have decided that it's at Mariette's. I think you panicked when she caught you and you threw the rolling pin meaning to scare her away, but not hurt her."

Bobby Ray's heart was pounding so hard he was afraid it was going to race right up his throat.

"Here's my plan," he continued. "When I go back to Mariette's, we're going to take every remaining block of butter in her fridge and melt it down until we find whatever it is you're looking for. And when we do, your jig is up. This is all coming to a close, anyway, Bobby Ray. I can help you," he said. "You go ahead and come clean now and we'll sort all of this out. I'll personally back Uncle Mackie and his goons off you and make sure that, as far as they're concerned, your debt is paid."

For the briefest second Bobby Ray was tempted to do exactly as Jack Martin said. He painted a pretty picture of redemption and escape… But, ultimately,

Bobby Ray knew he was here to do a job and his job wasn't to save his skin—it was to save Mariette's. He might have figured everything out, but he didn't have any proof. And until he had proof, Bobby Ray had time to try and sort things out himself.

When it became clear that Bobby Ray wasn't going to say anything, Jack sighed. "The hard way, then? I figured as much."

He reached into his pocket and handed Bobby Ray a wad of folded bills. Bobby Ray looked down and shock detonated through him. They were hundreds.

"Find somewhere to sleep besides your car," he said. "You look dead on your feet, probably from constantly looking over your shoulder. And pick a motel with laundry and room service. A little sleep, some clean clothes and a decent meal will do you a world of good." He handed him something else. "Here's my card. Call me if you change your mind. My cell is on there. No matter what happens, the offer stands, kid."

He clapped him on the back and then turned and walked away. Bobby Ray stood there for what felt like an eternity looking at the money that had just been put in his hand.

For the first time in his life he genuinely didn't know what to think.

"Why are you doing this?" he hollered to Jack's retreating form.

Jack paused, seemingly looking at something that Bobby Ray couldn't see. "Because it's the right thing to do and I don't think people have always done the right thing by you," he said. He paused. "And you remind me of someone."

10

"HEY, JAY," MARIETTE heard Jack say from her vantage point in the kitchen.

"Jack!" Livvie all but shouted. "Do you like chocolate?" she asked.

"I do," he told her, sounding only marginally startled at the out of the blue question.

"Good, 'cause Mariette made some special ones today, only she wouldn't let me have one. I don't know why. I've been good and only had one cookie."

Before this could deteriorate any further, Mariette hurried forward. "I'm making special ones for you, too, Livvie," she said, slinging an arm around the girl. "Come with me, please." She steered her toward the kitchen. "I've got a special job for you."

Predictably, Livvie's eyes lit up. The word *special* always had that effect on her. It made the car commercials—who were always having "specials"—particularly entertaining for her. Mariette shot Jack a significant look and jerked her head toward the kitchen, silently beckoning him to follow her. She was so glad that he'd gotten back in time to see this.

Looking intrigued at her admittedly odd behavior, Jack followed her around the counter and into the kitchen. "You are going to be so glad that you got here in time," she said, practically bubbling with expectation. She turned to Livvie. "I want you to take these to Charlie and Jay. Jay gets the duck plate, okay?"

Jack frowned. "The duck plate?"

"It's got a duck on it, see?" she said, a little impatiently.

Livvie nodded. "Jay gets the duck plate. Charlie gets the flowers."

"Right. Once you've given them their plates, I want you to come back—right back—to the kitchen. I have another special job for you." She pointed to a tray of un-iced sugar cookies. Icing cookies was one of Livvie's favorite things in the world to do. "You're going to take care of those for me, okay? We'll call them the Livvie Specials."

She clapped delightedly. "Livvie Specials! I like that!"

Mariette knew she would.

"Okay," she said, handing her helper the plates. "Hurry," she said. "Jay gets the duck plate," she repeated.

Smiling delightedly, Livvie took off.

Jack arched a brow. "Want to tell me what's going on? You're acting all…stealthy," he said, looking mildly impressed.

Having practically slung the plates down in front of Jay and Charlie, Livvie came running back into the kitchen and took up her icing bag. She was instantly engrossed. Mariette grabbed Jack's hand and hurried forward. "Do what I do," she said. "And be quiet."

Mariette dropped down into a low crouch and duck-walked to the best position behind the case. She'd purposely shifted things around in the case so that she'd have a better view.

"What the hell?" Jack hissed, his brows climbing nearly to his hairline.

Mariette shot him a warning glance and put her finger to her lips, the international sign for "shush." Once she was in a good position, she motioned for Jack to get closer and whispered, "Watch this."

"This feels wrong," he said. "I—"

"Shut up," she whispered fiercely. Like he'd never spied on anyone before. Honestly. "Trust me."

"I don't care if you're hungry or not," Mariette heard Charlie say. "Mariette made a special treat for the two of us, so just eat it."

He made a face and pushed the plate away. "I'll save it for later," he said. "I'm sure she won't mind."

Oh, yes, she would, Mariette thought.

"That's made with special chocolate," Charlie told

him. "It's supposed to enhance your sexual performance."

Jay went comically still and beside her Jack sniggered.

"I wasn't aware there was a problem," Jay said, darting a nervous look around the deserted dining room.

Charlie popped a bite in her mouth and groaned. "But the best can still be made better," she said, pulling a delicate shrug. "I was just more curious to see if it would work, but if it makes you uncomfortable or you're not into it, then that's fine."

"No, no," Jay said, picking up the little egg. "If eating sexual chocolate will make you happy, then I'm happy to oblige." He bit into it and winced. "What the—" He peered at the egg, then frowned at Charlie. "There's paper in here."

"Oh," Charlie said a little too innocently. "Mine didn't have that. You ought to see what it says." She leaned forward.

Mariette was practically shaking with anticipation, her smile so wide it hurt. She grabbed Jack's hand again and squeezed.

Looking adorably uncertain, Jay withdrew the little piece of paper and opened it up. A puzzled frown moved across his brow while he tried to figure out what he was looking at. Then he sucked in a harsh breath and his gaze shot to Charlie. "Congratulations, Daddy," he said, reading the little note at the bottom of the ultrasound picture. "Is this what— Are you— Are we—"

Tears glistened in Charlie's eyes and, smiling, she nodded.

The chair Jay was sitting on fell to the floor as he vaulted up from the table and swept Charlie up. He lifted her completely off the ground and whirled her around. He was laughing delightedly, an expression of pure joy in his face.

"Put me down," Charlie gasped. "You're going to make us sick." She glanced toward the counter. "You can stop hiding now."

Mariette and Jack popped up from behind the counter and Jay's eyes widened in shock. "Did you know?" he asked.

"Only because she couldn't stop herself from telling it," Mariette told him, laughing, too. What a beautiful moment and she'd been a part of it.

An odd expression on his face, Jack squeezed her hand and murmured a thank-you. "The egg had to be your idea. Brilliant." He walked over to Jay and offered him one of those handshake hugs men did. "Congratulations," he told him. "You'll make a fine father."

Jay nodded and slung an arm around Charlie. "I'm sure she'll have me whipped into shape before the baby is born." He blinked and looked down at her. "When will the baby be born?"

"October," Charlie told him.

"October," he repeated wonderingly. "We're having a baby in October."

Jay cast a fond look at his sister. "Go celebrate this news with your husband," he said. "I'm not leaving again today."

A hopeful light gleamed in Charlie's gaze. "You sure?"

He nodded. "I'm sure."

Charlie shrugged and darted a look at Mariette. "Thank you," she said, her eyes still wet.

"Anytime," Mariette told her.

Charlie snagged her purse, the ultrasound photo and the last bite of chocolate off her plate, then hurried back to Jay's side. She threaded her fingers through his as though her hand in his was the most natural thing in the world.

And it was, for them, Mariette realized.

"Does that chocolate really enhance sexual performance?" she heard Jay ask as they strolled out the door.

Charlie laughed delightedly. "I guess we'll see, won't we?"

Jack waited until they were gone, then turned to look at her. His expression was still on lockdown, but she detected a hint of approval for her part and that little bit of admiration burrowed into her heart and bloomed. "That was a great thing you just did."

Mariette grinned, toed a loose piece of rubber on

the mat behind the counter. "It felt good," she said. "They're so in love."

"I know." He grimaced, shot her a conspiratorial smile. "It's a little sickening, isn't it?"

Mariette felt her eyes round. "No," she said, feigning outrage.

He merely stared at her.

She huffed a breath. "Okay, just a little."

Jack laughed, the sound low and husky. "I knew you were a girl after my own heart."

If she didn't get control of herself, she imagined that was what she was going to be after—his heart. In the meantime, she'd just have to make do with the rest of him. A shudder racked her frame as desire spiked. In an instant she remembered the feel of his lips against her own, the way he tasted against her tongue, the way his skin felt beneath her mouth.

Jack's attention suddenly shifted to his cell phone. He checked the display, frowned and then looked up at her. "Who is Nathaniel, why will he be here at six and why am I supposed to take care of him for you?"

Mariette swore. "I need to check on Livvie," she said and made a beeline for the kitchen. It wouldn't put him off, but it would delay him a minute, anyway.

Damn Charlie. Pregnant or not, Mariette could throttle her. While the idea of having Jack convince Nathaniel to leave her alone satisfied some sort of primal cavewoman revenge gene, she really didn't think it was necessary. Yes, he'd been an ass and yes, it had been humiliating. But she wasn't heartbroken and she could fight her own battles.

She'd been doing it her whole life, hadn't she?

Furthermore, she was grimly afraid she'd like it too much, having Jack Martin in her corner.

And, though there were many pleasures she imagined she and Jack would enjoy, that one was somehow more significant, held more emotional appeal than was strictly good for her.

She'd do well to remember that.

"Mariette," Jack called, immediately falling in behind her. "What's Charlie talking about?"

"Oh, that's lovely," Mariette told Livvie, peering over the girl's shoulder. She gave her a squeeze. "You're doing a great job."

"Mariette," he repeated, less patiently.

She glanced up. "It's nothing," she said, blinking innocently. As if he'd fall for that. "It's not a problem."

"Charlie seems to think he's a problem," he said. He frowned, sighed heavily and pulled his phone from his waist again. "I guess I'll just have to call her and interrupt their romantic celebratory dinner and—"

She snatched the phone out of his hand. He was so shocked it took a moment for him to react. "What the hell—"

"I'll give it back," she said, looking at her hand as though she wasn't sure it belonged to her. "Just don't call her."

"Fine," he said. She handed the phone back to him. "Who is Nathaniel?" Jack asked. He had a terrible suspicion that he wasn't going to like this answer and the black cloud of rage settling on his brain was making it seize up. Ridiculous, he told himself. He shouldn't get this spun out over an ex-boyfriend and yet… He genuinely felt like hitting something.

Livvie made a face. "Nathanial used to be Mariette's boyfriend, but she kicked him to the curb."

Mariette gasped. "Livvie! Who told you such a thing?"

"Dillon," she said, as if it should be obvious. "Dillon didn't like Nathaniel, either. He said he had mean eyes." She put another misshapen heart on another cookie. "I didn't notice his mean eyes, but he was a brown. Not a pretty brown like chocolate. A yucky brown, like mud. Or poop."

Jack felt his lips twitch and his gaze tangled with Mariette's shocked and embarrassed one. "He doesn't sound like I would like him, either, Livvie."

"You wouldn't," Livvie said. "He's not a nice man. He only pretends to be. He's good at fooling people, but the colors don't lie."

Mariette winced and rubbed a finger between her brows, as though staving off a headache. "Livvie, you'd better get your things together. Your mom will be here soon."

Livvie placed a final dot on a cookie with flourish and then smiled down at her handiwork. "There you go, Mariette. Livvie's specials," she announced proudly.

Mariette smiled tiredly and hugged her. "Yes, they are."

Livvie buried her head into Mariette's neck, a glowing smile on her face. "I love you, Mariette."

"I love you, too, sweetheart," she murmured, pressing a kiss to the girl's temple.

He smiled softly, touched at the scene. He'd been seeing a lot of mutually adoring looks lately. Between Mariette and Livvie, Charlie and Jay.

Mariette pulled back and glanced down at the girl. "Livvie, why didn't you tell me about Nathaniel's color? You've never mentioned that before."

"I kept hoping it would change. Sometimes they do," she said. "And Momma told me not to meddle," she added, a frown creasing her otherwise smooth brow. "You aren't mad at me, are you, Mariette?"

"Of course not," she said. "I could never be mad at you," Mariette told her, giving her a squeeze. "You're my special Livvie."

Livvie beamed up at her. "You're my special Mariette." The bell on the front door rang, signaling a customer. "I bet that's Mom," she said. "She's always early."

"Livvie," a feminine voice called.

"Told ya," Livvie announced. "See you tomorrow, Mariette. Bye, Jack!"

Jack told her goodbye and then watched her leave. "Sounds like Livvie is a really good judge of character," he remarked. "You should probably start vetting all your boyfriends through her."

She winced and started cleaning up. He liked the way she moved, determined and purposeful with an economy of movement that was graceful, almost regal. "That's not a bad idea, actually."

"What's this Nathaniel been doing?" He tried not to mangle the words, but, at her sharp look, wasn't altogether sure that he'd succeeded. It was ridiculous how much this was eating him up. Of course, she'd had boyfriends before. She was twenty-seven. She was beautiful. It was completely natural and completely normal.

And yet, the idea of her kissing anyone—touching anyone—the way she was kissing and touching him last night made him want to howl like a wounded animal and break things. He was jealous, Jack realized with a jolt of absolute horror.

Jealous of someone he'd never met, never seen.

All because he'd been someone Mariette had been involved with.

Dread ballooned in his belly. Oh, this was bad, Jack thought. This was very, very bad.

He'd never been jealous of anything or anyone

before, had never had reason to be. If a girl he liked chose another guy—which, to be fair, hadn't happened all that often—then he just moved on and found another one. Girls were girls. If one wasn't interested there was always one who would be.

Mariette wiped down the counter, sweeping cookie crumbs into her hands. Her mink-colored hair had been braided in a long rope that hung down on the side of her neck and curled provocatively around her breast. She wore another long-sleeve T-shirt and another pair of equally figure-flattering jeans. Small pearl studs gleamed from her ears and a gold locket dangled around her neck. He didn't have to open it to know that it would contain a picture of her mother.

A thought struck and he blinked. "Where's your aunt?" he wanted to know. "The one your mother named you after?"

She paused and darted him a strange look. "She's in Florida," she said. "She's retired from the state. She worked thirty years for the Treasury Department." She grinned, seemingly perplexed. "That was a bit random. I thought you were still stuck on Nathaniel."

His mood blackened at the reminder. "I guess the question isn't whether I'm still stuck on Nathaniel," he said, trying hard to sound calm and rational, neither of which he was at the moment. "It's whether or not you're still stuck on him."

She snorted as if the idea repulsed her. "No," she said, shooting him a level look. "I'm not."

Jack nodded once. "Good."

Her lips twitched, probably at his utterly ridiculous behavior. He didn't like being jealous. It made him feel strange, God help him, vulnerable even. It completely unsettled him.

She unsettled him.

Because that thought was too revealing and begged a lot of personal exploration involving feelings and emotions and everything else he'd managed to avoid the bulk of his entire adult life, Jack forced himself to change the subject altogether.

To one he knew she wasn't going to like.

Bobby Ray.

"We need to melt down all your remaining butter," Jack announced.

She started and looked up at him. Her pale gray eyes widened in shock. "What?"

Jack recounted everything he'd learned that day and concluded with his trip to the dairy. "I let him know that Mackie's boys were going to stay at the motel and that the clerk I talked to today was going to see to his things so that he wouldn't lose them. He knows I know there's a connection and he's terrified. I told him that I'd help him, that I'd make sure the debt was considered paid and that I'd back them off him, but he just doesn't trust me enough to let me do it. I'm sure he thinks that if he comes clean I'm going to haul him off to jail."

Mariette leaned against the counter, seemingly deep in thought. A line puckered her brow. "It could have been him," she said. "He's certainly the right height and build."

"He's obviously gotten into something he's not capable of getting out of on his own."

She looked up at him. "And you think that whatever he's taking from Audwin is hidden in the butter?"

Jack shrugged. "It's the only thing that makes sense, Mariette. He has no access to anyone or anything else. He's gotten snarled up with a mean-spirited bookie who's roughed him up once. He's shaking in his boots. So terrified that he won't go home." He passed a hand over his face. "And the kid looks terrible. Pale, drawn and sick. He's dirty, he hasn't bathed. I gave him some money for a room and told him to get his clothes cleaned and have a good meal. Maybe if he has a moment of safety he'll come to his senses."

She glanced up sharply and her expression softened. "You did? You gave him money?"

From the way she was looking at him one would think that he'd managed world peace or something equally impressive. Incredibly, he felt heat rise in his face. "I feel sorry for him," he said. "You were right.

He's a good kid who needs to be shown the better side of humanity. All he's seen is its worst."

Mariette tossed the washcloth in her hand aside, walked over to him, grabbed him by the shirt with both hands and yanked him down. Her smiling lips met his in a kiss that made the hair on his scalp tingle and the sensation moved with startling rapidity all the way down his body, clear to the soles of his feet.

Well, all righty, then.

Should he tell her about the old lady he'd helped across the street, too?

He quickly picked her up and set her on the counter behind him, then moved in between her legs. She wrapped her arms around his neck and her legs around his waist and pushed her sweet tongue into his mouth, inflaming him. She smelled like vanilla and sugar and she was achingly soft where she should be soft and firm where she should be firm. Her hair was cool against the backs of his hands and he fisted them in it the way he'd thought about doing the first time he'd ever seen her.

She left off his mouth and rained kisses down his cheek, along his jaw and down his neck. She sucked a little skin into her mouth and the response that hit his dick meant that she might as well have wrapped her lips around it instead.

He pushed up against her, tugged her shirt from the waistband of her jeans and slipped his hands up the small of her back, tracing the fluted spine with his thumbs.

She shivered and let go a low mewl of pleasure, then scooted even closer to the edge of the counter, putting the heart of her sex against the ridge of his arousal. She squirmed against him and he answered with a determined flex of his hips.

Another little gasp of delight slipped between her lips and he ate it, feasting on her mouth. Seemingly desperate to touch him, as well, she burrowed her hands beneath his sweater and skimmed her fingers along his sides. Her touch was soft and cool, but the havoc it wreaked in his body was anything but.

He was burning up.

So hot for her he should have flames spurting out of the top of his head. His head was ringing so hard he thought he heard bells.

The bell. Shit.

"You've got a customer," he said.

She arched against him again. "I don't care," she breathed against him.

Jack chuckled, gratified. "But you will when they leave." He reluctantly pulled away from her.

"Well, I see you have moved on," a male voice drawled from the doorway. Mariette instantly stiffened and Jack's gaze shifted to the direction of the speaker. He was medium height, medium build, nicely dressed and smug.

Jack instantly hated him.

"Let me guess," Jack said. "This must be Nathaniel."

Mariette glared at the intruder. "I told you not to come back."

His thin nostrils flared. "And I told you that you were being ridiculous."

Jack laughed, though the sound was not humorous. "Now I see what Charlie meant." He pressed a kiss against her forehead. "Excuse me a moment," he said and straightened. The look he sent Nathanial would have made a less-arrogant man quail. But this one was more than arrogant—he was stupid, as well.

Jack strolled forward, smiling all the while. If the idiot had one grain of sense he'd be afraid, since Jack desperately wanted to hit him. He refrained, but it wasn't easy. "She is *not* ridiculous," Jack said, his voice a low lethal growl. "She's *perfect* and she is finished with you." Jack wrapped his hand around the back of Nathaniel's neck, causing the moron to yelp like the little dog he was, then turned him around and hauled him back out the front door, then shoved him onto the sidewalk. "Do not come back," he said. "Ever. You are banned."

Strictly speaking, he didn't have the authority to ban anyone from her shop, but under the circumstances he hoped she wouldn't mind. He turned then and she was standing behind the counter, her eyes wide, her smile wider. She shook her head.

"I'm perfect, am I?"

He'd said it in the heat of the moment, but realized just then that he knew it was true. As far as he was concerned, yes, she was perfect.

And he was doomed.

"Lock that door, would you?" She turned to leave, then shot a look at him over her shoulder. "Then come upstairs. We have some unfinished business to complete."

And with another little smile, she left.

Slay a dragon, get the girl, Jack thought. And this girl was more than worth it.

11

MARIETTE HAD NEVER pegged herself for a woman who needed a grand gesture or one who liked for men to fight over her, or even be willing to fight over her, for that matter.

But watching the thundercloud of supreme displeasure descend over Jack's previously sleepy-looking, sexy countenance had been positively... thrilling.

She should be ashamed of herself, really, but couldn't muster the required humility.

She'd felt his anger rise up—could scarcely believe that Nathanial hadn't noticed it—and when her ex had made the "ridiculous" comment, whatever control Jack had attempted to maintain snapped.

Even his laugh—that little dark chuckle—had been rife with pure, white-hot fury. The atmosphere in the room had changed so much she'd felt the little hairs on the back of her arms rise up.

And Nathaniel—she inwardly shook her head—dumb-ass Nathaniel, didn't have sense enough to retreat. To run. He just stood there. She snickered. Until Jack snatched him up and hauled him forcibly out of her shop and onto the sidewalk.

And Jack had done that for her—because she'd been insulted. Because he thought she was perfect.

It was a caveman tactic to be sure, but she'd *loved* it.

Mariette had no more than unlocked the door when she heard him pounding up the stairs behind her. She turned in time to watch him bend down and toss her over his shoulder.

She squealed and gasped as her feet left the ground. "What are you doing? Put me down!"

He went unerringly to her bedroom and tumbled her onto the bed. "If that's what you want," he said, coming down next to her. His mouth instantly found hers, taking her lips in a deep, breath-stealingly electrifying kiss. She felt it all the way down to her toes, where they curled in the shoes she hadn't had time to take off. She did now, kicking them onto the floor, where they landed with a decided *thump*.

She wrapped her arms more tightly around him, pushing her hands into hair. She loved his hair, the silky way it slipped through her fingers. She caressed the soft skin behind his ear, relished the feel of his hard, long body pressed to hers.

He sucked her bottom lip into his mouth and

groaned low. "You taste so good," he said, kissing her again, making love to her mouth.

Mariette tugged at his sweater until he drew back enough to let her pull it over his head. She cast it aside and then looked greedily at him. Smooth, supple skin, the muscular curve of his shoulder, the flare of muscles at his sides, tapering into a lean, hard waist. Blond hairs whorled over his pecs and a treasure trail arrowed low and beneath the waistband of his jeans.

He was absolutely breathtaking. The best specimen of a man she'd ever seen. She trailed her fingers over his chest, his flesh hot and soft, then bent forward and touched her tongue to a male nipple.

He shuddered. Quaked.

And the power instantly went to her head. She did it again, slipping her fingers along his back, down his spine, then nipped at the ruched tip and he sucked in a hiss between his teeth.

Rather than take that lying down, as it were, Jack immediately relieved her of her shirt. His eyes feasted on her bare flesh, making her feel beautiful and wanted, treasured. She reached up and popped the catch on her bra, opening it for him. He bent forward and nudged one cup aside, then circled the globe with his nose, breathing her in. She could feel his hot breath against her skin, raising gooseflesh as it grazed her aching nipple. A chord of longing tightened in her core, and she arched up against him, desperate and needy.

Her breath came in sharp little puffs that were almost embarrassing they were so loud, but she couldn't seem to help herself. When it came to this level of desire, she was way out of her depth. It was beyond anything she'd ever experienced, ever imagined possible. Every cell in her body was clamoring for him—his taste, his scent, his skin on hers, his skin *in* hers.

His mouth closed over her nipple, snatching the breath from her lungs as he suckled deep, his tongue rasping over the hardened peak.

She turned, trying to get closer to him and slid her hand down his belly until she found the button at his waist. He drew a sharp breath when her fingers brushed against the top of his penis, which had escaped its enclosure, as it were.

Sweet heaven, Mariette thought, as she lowered his zipper and he sprung free into her waiting hand. He moved to the other breast, his own clever fingers expertly undoing her jeans, as well. She lifted up so that he could work the jeans down over her hips, then kicked them aside with more haste than grace.

His hands were suddenly all over her, sliding along her side, over her middle and then into her weeping folds. The first brush of his fingers against her sensitive flesh made her inhale deeply and he took that opportunity to find her mouth once more, eating the sigh that came with the exhalation of gratified air.

He dallied expertly between her legs and she worked the long hard length of him against her palm and all the while her skin burned up and shivered and desire alternately weighted her limbs and made her restless. She felt as though she was going to die if he didn't take her, that she'd die when he did and she just wanted, she just needed…him.

"Please," she whispered brokenly, not ashamed to beg.

He drew back, snagged a condom from his wallet and swiftly rolled it into place, then positioned himself between her thighs. He was huge, much bigger than she'd realized. He nudged high, sliding his thickness along her folds, coating himself in her juices before slipping back and prodding her entrance. He gave a gentle push and she inhaled, desperately wanting him more deeply inside her.

"I don't want to hurt you," he said, his face a mask of tight control.

"I'm not going to break," she said, dragging her legs back and opening more widely for him. She arched up, taking a little more of him in and she watched him set his jaw, the muscles jump in his cheek.

He pushed again, just a little, and stars danced behind her lids. He waited, allowing her to stretch and accommodate his size, then she arched up again, taking a little bit more of him.

Sweat beaded his brow and his forearms were lined with taut, distended veins. Any other man would have plowed right ahead, without a care for whether or not she was hurt, but this one... This one would hurt himself before hurting her. An aching swelled in her chest, a tenderness she'd never experienced before.

Mariette bent forward and kissed his chest, his throat. "Come here," she said, pulling him down closer. She found his mouth, kissed him deeply and felt him relax more fully. She arched again, felt him slide in a little deeper, and then with a deep, resigned sigh he breathed right into her mouth—into her very soul—and he pushed in and filled her up.

Literally.

It was indescribably perfect, the way he felt inside of her.

She tightened around him, sighed once more, and then arched up, savoring every ridge, every vein, the engorged head of his penis. She could feel it all in individual parts when he pushed into her and the sensation was nothing short of exquisite.

Once he was certain that he wasn't going to hurt her, Jack became less hesitant and more determined. Now that he'd invaded her body, he was going to make it submit to his will.

And she would, she knew, all too readily.

He plunged in and out of her, a slow, steady rhythm that stoked a fire that was already blazing out of control. Mariette could feel the first flash of release building in her sex, deep in her womb, and she welcomed that reward, needed it more desperately than she'd ever needed anything before. She arched up against him, meeting him thrust for thrust and tightened her feminine muscles around him.

Jack's breath came in hard little puffs and he angled deeper and higher. Her aching breasts absorbed the force of his thrusts, bouncing on her chest, and her belly felt as if it was going to hit her backbone if she breathed any harder. She wrapped her arms around him, licked a path along his neck and to his shoulder.

He quaked against her, pounded harder. Higher, harder, faster, he plunged in and out of her, his tautened balls hitting her sensitive flesh with every brutal thrust.

The orgasm ultimately hit her without warning.

One minute she'd been savoring him—the way he fit inside of her, the way he looked on top of her, the determined glint in his heavy-lidded eyes.

The next she was flying apart, a long, keening cry tearing from her throat. She spasmed hard around him and every muscle in her body seized up and then released, leaving her feeling melted and sated and unbelievably happy.

MARIETTE'S TIGHT LITTLE BODY fisted around him over and over, her mouth opening in a cry of gratifying pleasure, her neck arched as she let the delight swell through her.

Dark hair against the down comforter, her sinfully carnal mouth carved into a blissed-out smile that he'd put on her face, her breasts rosy tipped and pouting...

She was unequivocally the most beautiful woman he'd ever seen.

Or would ever see again, he knew.

Jack buried himself to the hilt again, absorbing the absolute glory of her perfect body. She was hot and soft and tight—so *damned* tight—and he'd been terrified of hurting her, of making a move that would result in her pain, but she'd taken him in, inch by inch, degree by degree until he could feel nothing but her...and that was all that mattered.

Her soft hands glided over him now, greedy and slow, as though she couldn't get enough of him, either, as though she needed him—*this*—as much as he did. She tightened around him, bent forward and slid her wicked tongue against his throat again, along his jaw. He loved her mouth, the feel of it, the taste of it, the things she did with it. To him.

She drew her legs back, anchoring around his waist once more and her feet curved around the twin globes of his ass, urging him on. He heard her gasp, make another little mewl of satisfaction and felt her contract around him once more.

"Oh, no," she said, thrashing beneath him. "I can't— It's too much— I—" She screamed again, her voice low and hoarse and wilted, into the mattress beneath him. Her tight channel closed around him, once, twice, a third time.

He came hard.

His vision blackened around the edges, his head spun and he shook so hard he was afraid his suddenly weakened limbs wouldn't support him.

Release racked through him, twisting through his body like a sensual tornado of feeling. Pleasure, relief, ecstasy and something else, something altogether more tender, more significant and more terrifying than anything he'd ever felt before. He seated himself as far into her as he could go, letting the last of the tremors run through him, then looked down into her upturned face.

Her eyes were closed, the lashes longer and curlier than he'd realized, her cheeks flushed, lips swollen from his kisses. A soft smile, one of absolute contentment, shaped her sinful mouth. She opened her eyes then and he watched the pupils dilate, adjusting to the light. They weren't merely gray, Jack decided. They were silver. And they had the power to look right through him, to lay him bare and leave him open. Much as the thought sent a dagger of dread into his chest, the thing that scared him the most—made him nearly ill when he thought about it—was the idea of not being able to do this again.

He bent forward and pressed a kiss to her lips, slid a finger reverently down the side of her face.

This girl was going to be the end of him, Jack thought. But if so, he'd come to a better end than most.

12

"THAT'S THE LAST OF IT," Mariette said, coming out of the walk-in fridge.

Wearing only pajama bottoms and a puzzled look, Jack arched a brow. "You're sure?"

She nodded and heaved a sigh. "Yes. You've melted all of my butter. I have no idea how I'm going to bake tomorrow," she said, looking forlornly at all that wasted buttery goodness.

Jack winced, his face a mask of utter perplexity. "I was certain that we'd find it," he said. "I know that he's hidden it here. He didn't even try to deny it, Mariette. He didn't even bother."

Mariette plopped up onto a bar stool and snagged one of Livvie's Specials to munch on. Though they'd ordered takeout and she'd eaten plenty, she was still starving. Her lips curled as her gaze drifted down the masculine slope of Jack's shoulders, the sheer magnificence of his muscled frame.

Of course, she'd no doubt burned a lot of calories this evening. Sex would do that for a girl. And lots of blistering-hot, sweaty, splendid sex would do even more.

Mariette couldn't remember a time when she'd ever—*ever*—had a multiple orgasm. Of course she'd heard about the legendary double O, but it had always escaped her. Quite frankly, she'd never achieved orgasm through sex alone. She'd always required a little more…stimulation. The fact that Jack Martin had made her sing the Hallelujah twice without using any digits or battery-operated devices was nothing short of a sexual miracle for her.

He. Was. Awesome.

And huge. And *straight*. As a friggin' arrow.

Even now, just looking at him, made something warm and hot slither into her belly. Her breasts pebbled behind her nightshirt—she'd forgone the bra— and she felt a twinge of remembered pleasure echo in her womb. She could take him again, Mariette realized. Right here, right now. In fact, she grimly suspected that she would always want him, crave him, even, and the idea was as pleasant as it was disturbing.

She didn't want to need him. She didn't want to need anybody, Mariette thought, because needing led to heartache. Unfortunately, when it came to Jack Martin she didn't think she was going to have a choice. He…just made her feel good. He made her body hum and her heart—an organ that had no business being involved in this, considering that she barely knew him—sing. He was smart and funny and honorable and she didn't give a damn whether the people of Pennyroyal thought their golden boy was tarnished.

If you asked her, he was perfect…too.

When he'd told her tonight that he'd given Bobby Ray the money for a motel room and had offered to help the boy—despite believing that he was guilty of something here—something inside of her had just… snapped. He'd reviewed all of the facts, taken the time to find out what was going on with the kid, and then extended an offer that Mariette was sure the boy had never been given before—mercy.

And when he'd kicked Nathanial out… Well, that had just been icing on the cake.

Jack Martin was unlike any man she'd ever met before and she instinctively knew she'd never meet one better. Irrational, considering her track record? Possibly, but she knew it all the same. He was different. He made her feel different. He made her want to believe that she could have what Jay and Charlie had, the kind of love that didn't ask for anything in return. That just…*was*.

A possessiveness she'd never imagined herself capable of burst through her, momentarily taking her aback. The idea of anyone else touching him—of *him* touching anyone else the way he'd just touched her—made her mind turn black with rage and recoil.

"Are you all right?" Jack asked, a concerned line between his brows. "I'll replace your butter," he said. "I'll call Audwin right now and go get it if you'd like."

Mariette blinked, trying to pull her thoughts together. "That's all right," she said. "If you don't mind if I work for a little while, I'll go ahead and get everything ready for tomorrow." That way she could save a portion of it anyway.

Jack swore. "Aren't you tired?" he asked. "You've been up since three and I was under the impression that you hadn't slept very well."

That was true, she'd admit. After their marathon kissing session in the kitchen she'd been even more wound up than she'd been before she'd gone in there. His fault, she thought, heaving a fatalistic sigh. She imagined lots of things in the near future were going to be his fault. She smiled anyway and hopped down from the chair.

"That's true," she said. "But I find myself strangely energized."

His lips slid into a slow grin. "Really? Sex energizes you?" He shook his head. "Could you be any more perfect?"

"No," Mariette quipped. She dipped a finger in the warm butter and sucked it off her finger, her eyes widening appreciatively. "That's good stuff. Everything is better with butter."

She looked over at Jack and his mouth had gone a bit slack. He blinked. Swallowed. "I'm sorry. Could you do that again?"

She laughed. "Men are so visual," she said.

"I know," he told her with a pointed look. "That's why I asked you to do it again."

She pulled a bowl from the rack above her head and started measuring out ingredients. "Don't you have anything to do?" she asked. "A file you should be looking over or something?"

He hopped up on another counter, crossed his arms over his chest and studied her. "No. I know who our culprit is," he said. "I've just got to try to convince him to come clean before anything happens to him."

"Why do you have to wait?" Mariette asked. She dumped a pound of sugar into the bowl. "You know who's harassing him. Go whack 'em or whatever."

He chuckled softly under his breath. "Whack 'em? I'm not a mob boss, Mariette."

She measured the butter and dumped it the bowl, then shoved it under the mixer. "I know that, smart-ass. I just meant do to them what you've already told him you'd do. Make them leave him alone. Once you've done that, then he'll trust you and he won't have any reason to continue doing whatever it is he's doing."

Jack was thoughtful for a moment. "You know," he said after a minute, "that's a good idea."

She shot him a droll smile. "Occasionally, I have them."

He grinned. "I didn't mean it like that. Making Uncle Mackie and his muscle back off of Bobby Ray would certainly take the pressure off, that's for sure." He winced. "I don't know what he's taken from Audwin, but that's probably not going to be anything I can fix."

Mariette added eggs and vanilla into the bowl. "Like me, Audwin has a soft spot for Bobby Ray. Whatever it is that he's done, I think Audwin would ultimately forgive him."

Jack paused, snuck one of Livvie's Specials and chewed thoughtfully. "I think you're probably right. But Bobby Ray isn't used to being given any grace. Convincing him to tell the truth isn't going to be easy."

Mariette started measuring the flour in. "If anyone can do it, I'm sure you can."

He was quiet for so long she turned to look at him. His expression was strange, a mix between wondering and haunted.

Mariette frowned. "Did I say something wrong?" she asked.

He chuckled, cleared his throat. "No," he said. "You said something so right it took me off guard, that's all."

Mariette smiled tentatively. "I have no idea what you mean by that," she said.

"Good," he quipped, passing a hand over his face. "Because I don't understand it, either."

"You seem to be adjusting well," she remarked, hoping that she wasn't crossing some invisible booby-trapped line that was going to blow up in her face.

"To what?"

"Being a civilian," she said. She continued to work, purposely didn't look at him.

"I suppose," he said, casting her a speculative look that made her unaccountably nervous. "What all has Charlie told you?"

Mariette darted him a look. "What makes you think she's told me anything?"

"Please," he said, as though she'd insulted him. "You've met my sister. She's bossy, opinionated and has no brain-to-mouth filter." A dry bark of laughter erupted from his throat. "She's filled your ears full, hasn't she?"

Damn, she should have kept her mouth shut. She had no desire to start a war between brother and sister. "She's sung your praises," she said. "If that's what you mean by filling my ears full."

He swore. "She told you about Baghdad, didn't she? Come clean, Mariette. What else did she say?"

"She said that you were valedictorian of your class, the star quarterback for your high school football team and that girls threw their panties at you when you walked down Main Street."

He guffawed, filched another cookie. "Bullshit."

"Well, I might have interpreted that last part based on her 'town golden boy' comment, but otherwise it's all true." She withdrew a cupcake pan and started popping liners into the cups. "She adores you, you know. She thinks the sun rises and sets on you."

Still smiling, he got up and poured himself a glass of milk. "I know she loves me," he said. "And I love her, too. We've always been close."

Mariette sighed. "I can tell," she said. "I'm envious."

He paused. "I guess family was a little thin for you, wasn't it?"

"Just me, my mother and my aunt. My grandparents died when I was three—car accident. My aunt was so busy taking care of me and my mother that she never married or had children of her own. She's got a boyfriend now," she said, shooting him a smile. "It's cute. They play bingo together and are in the drama club in their retirement village."

"That sounds nice."

"I miss her," Mariette said and could hear the wistfulness in her own voice. "I go down for the holidays, usually."

"What part of Florida?"

"Tampa."

"I've always heard that's a nice area."

"It is. I love the ocean. Breathing it in, tasting the salt in the air."

"I haven't been in years," Jack said, a touch of disbelief in his voice.

Mariette looked up. "Why not?"

Another smile. "No time," he said. He grimaced. "War is hell."

She pulled a cup from the rack and started dipping the batter up. "I guess your family would have objected to you coming to the States and going to the beach instead of home."

"Er, yes," he said. "That would have gone over like a lead balloon."

"You've got time now," she pointed out.

"I do, don't I?"

She shot him another look. "Yes, you do. Being home is going to have its perks."

His gaze drifted over her face, lingered on her lips. "I've found one already."

Holy hell, Mariette thought. That look was hot enough to melt that butter all over again. She released a shuddering breath and made herself turn back to the task at hand. She felt his heat before he touched her and it was all she could do not to lean back and sink into him. And then she wondered what the hell was wrong with her. Why couldn't she lean back and sink into him? He lifted the hair off her neck and pressed a kiss to her nape.

"I love the way you smell, Mariette. It drives me crazy."

She shivered, relaxed more fully against him.

He placed another kiss just behind her ear, his breath fanning against her, then reached around and filled his hands with her breasts, massaged them through the shirt, tweaking her aching nipples. She pressed her rear end against him, arching up and felt him harden, his sex riding high against her rump.

She went boneless, her head becoming too heavy for her neck. "Jack, I—"

He shushed her, dipped a finger into the butter and put it to her mouth. "Suck it, Mariette," he whispered. "I want to feel your lips around me."

Oh, sweet hell.

She opened for him, taking his finger into her mouth.

He groaned into her ear, pressed against her. "Damn, woman, you're killing me."

She slid her tongue along the bottom of his finger, mimicking what she'd do to another part of him. "You asked me to," she said.

He chuckled softly and she turned her head, and found his mouth. The kiss was slow and deep, deliberate and thorough and the need she was certain was never going to leave her boiled up inside so quickly that she wondered if something was wrong with her internal thermometer. It couldn't be good for her to be this hot.

He sucked at her tongue, slid his big hands beneath her nightshirt and palmed her breasts once more. She rubbed her rump against him again, arched like a cat, then turned around, twined her arms around his neck and jumped up, wrapping her legs around his waist.

"Take me over there," she said, indicating the small love seat against the wall. "And then just take me."

And then just take me...

God help him, she was going to be the death of him, Jack thought as he did as she asked. He strode over to the little sofa and tumbled her onto her back.

"Oh, no," she said. "Like this." She nudged him into a sitting position and then straddled him. She dragged her shirt over her head, revealing pert, puckered breasts that begged for his kiss and a pair of panties that were so small they might as well be nonexistent.

He slid his hands over her back, relishing the feel of her and pulled a rosy bud into his mouth, suckling her deeply. She squirmed on top of him, then reached down and freed his shaft from his pajama bottoms and positioned it at her entrance. She slid her wet folds against him in a move so provocative, so bold and so damned wonderful he almost came right then. His eyes widened.

"Mariette, I don't have a condom down here."

"Neither do I," she said. "But I'm clean and protected. You?"

"Clean, yes."

"Works for me." She lifted her hips and slowly anchored herself on top of him, her tight, moist heat closing deliciously around him. She hissed low and slow, her eyes fluttering shut as though he felt too good, as though she needed him as much as he needed her.

She lifted again, sank again. Her ass was ripe and wonderful and he slid his hands over it possessively, fed at her breasts while she rode him. It was slow at first, deliberate and purposeful. But the harder he sucked on her, the harder she rode him and before long her hips were moving faster than he could suck. He squeezed her backside and bucked beneath her.

Her fingers scored his chest as she writhed on top of him, dark hair spilling over her shoulders, brushing her breasts, a thatch of equally dark curls at the apex of her thighs. The gentle flare of her hips, the concave belly, the firm thighs…

She was a goddess, a dream, a present he didn't even know he wanted.

And when she'd blithely told him that if anyone could convince Bobby Ray to do the right thing, then it would be him… Jack didn't know what had happened or why her vote of confidence had meant so much.

But it had.

She didn't doubt him. Believed in him.

He knew that his family still believed in him. Hell, even his fellow soldiers had after the accident. Any one of them would have gone out with him again. But until that moment Jack hadn't realized that he hadn't truly trusted himself, hadn't fully believed that he was still the same man. Still strong, still capable.

Still him.

Until *she'd* believed in him.

She swore and rode him harder, her tight little body closing around him. Her breath came in frantic little puffs, her face flushed pink. She sank her teeth into her bottom lip and then arched back and let go a sound that was so personal, so primal and so uninhibited, it set him off like a Roman candle. The release blasted from the back of his loins, shot through the heart of his dick and spilled into her.

He quaked with the strength of it. Shook.

It was the single most magnificent sensation of his life.

The world receded, time slowed to a crawl and even though he could hear his heart racing in his chest, even that seemed suddenly sluggish.

Jack Martin had been stealing kisses since kindergarten, making it to third base in junior high and had been regularly hitting it out of the park, so to speak, since his freshman year of high school.

He had never, not once, had unprotected sex.

His seed had never seen the inside of a woman. Until now.

He wanted to beat his chest and roar, wanted to scoop her up, haul her upstairs and do it all over again. He wanted to brand her somehow, let the world know that she was his and only his.

She framed his face with her hands, slid her fingers reverently along his jaw. Her gaze was tender and replete and rife with affection and something else…something more significant.

"You've ruined me for other men," she said, releasing a fatalistic sigh. She dropped her forehead against his. "I hope you're happy."

And he was.

13

MARIETTE WATCHED DILLON and Livvie from the doorway of the kitchen and felt a lump inexplicably swell in her throat. Both of their heads were bent low, almost touching, as Dillon hooked Livvie up with the promised ink. They were so sweet, so pure and so completely innocent it made her chest ache with joy.

She cast a glance at Charlie, who looked back at her with tears in her eyes. She laughed quietly and fanned her face. "I'm an emotional wreck," she said. "Bloody hormones."

Livvie laughed at something Dillon said and the boy leaned back in his chair, his chest puffed out, practically preening. He adored Livvie and the sentiment was wholly reciprocated.

Because she suspected she might be on to something like that herself—dare she even hope?—she knew her emotions were riding high on the surface.

And she didn't have any pregnancy hormones to blame, either.

She just had a hot former Army Ranger spending the night with her, bellying up to her back, making her middle go warm and squishy and her heart melt like a popsicle on the Fourth of July.

"What happened to all the butter?" Maggie wanted to know.

Mariette blushed, remembering the bit she'd licked off Jack's finger. She'd never look at butter the same, that was for damned sure.

"There was a problem with it," Mariette said evasively, unable to look anyone in the eye, most definitely Charlie who would know that something was up.

She was too perceptive by half, Mariette thought. And, while she didn't expect Charlie to be too broken up over the fact that Mariette had been sleeping—in the literal sense, as well—with her brother, it was nevertheless a conversation she didn't want to have.

"I need a bit more for the bread," Maggie told her. "Just to brush on the tops before I put the loaves in the oven."

"All right," Mariette told her. "I'll run upstairs and get some from my fridge."

She'd called Audwin this morning and told him she was going to need a delivery this afternoon and he'd promised to send Bobby Ray over later in the day. He'd apologized to Mariette—as though it were somehow his fault—and told her not to hesitate to contact him if she needed him. Dear man. He seemed so lost without Martha. No doubt Bobby Ray had been good company for him.

Mariette snagged all that she had and hurried back downstairs, then handed it over to Maggie. "This should tide us over until Bobby Ray comes by," she said.

Mariette had just made it to the door when Maggie made a disgusted harrumph. "There's something in this," she said.

Mariette whirled around, her heart pounding. "What?" She rushed forward and took the block of butter from Maggie's hands.

"Give me a knife, would you?" she asked.

Maggie handed it over and Mariette carefully cut away the part that housed the object. She set the rest of the block aside and worked on clawing away the remaining butter until she'd managed to see well enough to know what she had.

"A coin," Maggie said, surprised. "It looks like an old one, too." Her gaze met Mariette's. "Guess we know what the Butter Bandit was after."

Yes, she thought. They certainly did. She hollered for Charlie and snagged the phone to call Jack.

JACK HAD SPENT THE BETTER part of the day trying to find Uncle Mackie's goons, but had finally lucked out and found Uncle Mackie himself.

Behind a Porta-Potty, getting blown by a scrawny woman with bad skin.

"Leave," he told her. She scrambled up and darted away.

His sister had given him all the ammunition he needed on Uncle Mackie to bring the fat bastard to heel. Mackie was tall, but soft, with a beer belly, buckteeth—the few that he had, anyway—and mean, shrewd eyes.

It was almost better that he wasn't stupid, Jack thought. Perhaps he'd be smart enough to be scared.

"What the hell do you think you're doing?" he blustered, stowing his limp dick.

"Are you Mackie?" Jack asked. He knew he was, of course, but the man was so fond of the Uncle moniker, Jack knew he'd correct him.

"It's Uncle Mackie," he said.

Jack struck. He slammed his fist into the man's soft belly and when he doubled over, Jack twisted his arm up behind his back so hard that he heard it creak. That was for Bobby Ray, he thought. "You're no uncle of mine," he said, his tone lethal.

"You'd better get off me, boy," he said, breathing hard. "You don't know who you're messing with."

Jack pushed his arm up a little more. "As it happens, I do. You're the one who doesn't know who you're messing with. I'm a former Army Ranger with more skills and kills under my belt than you'd ever believe. I know a thousand different ways to hurt, maim, incapacitate and otherwise make you beg for death, you mean-spirited little bitch. I'm not a street thug, Mackie," Jack told him. "I'm a trained assassin, one of Uncle Sam's finest, and I've got *you*—" he gave him a little shake "—in my cross-hairs. I know that you're a misdemeanor away from a felony charge and my old man and grandfather were both with the Atlanta P.D. long enough to know who to talk to to see that you go away for a long, long time." He paused, could smell the fear on him. "Am I making myself clear?"

"Look, man, I don't want any trouble," he said, immediately backtracking. "What do you want?"

"I want you to absolve Bobby Ray Bishop of any debt and leave him the hell alone. If you or anyone associated with you comes within five miles of him—if I hear a single hair on his head has been touched or harmed in any way—I will come after you. I will hurt you. I will torture you." Jack shoved him to the ground and pulled the soap and sock from his back pocket and slowly assembled his weapon, the same one that had been used on Bobby Ray.

Mackie quailed and tried to scramble away, but Jack kicked him, preventing his escape. He took the sock and swung it hard against the man's back, thinking of poor skinny, scarred-up Bobby Ray with every strike.

Mackie howled with pain.

Jack did it again.

"Sucks when you're the one getting the beating, doesn't it, Mackie?" Jack asked conversationally. He swung again and again and ultimately had to make himself stop because he was enjoying it too much. But this was the only language a man like Mackie understood and Jack was fully capable of speaking it when he had to.

"Call them off," Jack said. "And stay away from Bobby Ray. Consider that *my* warning."

Jack turned and walked away, and left the man whimpering on the ground. It was fitting, he decided. That's what he'd done to Bobby Ray.

He'd just reached the car when his cell vibrated at his waist. He checked the display and smiled when he saw it was Mariette. "Hey," he said, pleasure winging through his chest.

"You were right," she said, her voice grim.

"I usually am, but about what this time?"

"I'd forgotten that I took a couple of loaves of butter upstairs," she said.

Every sense went on point. "And?"

"And I found an old coin in one of the loaves."

She sounded sick. "Mariette, we knew that he'd taken something. This doesn't change anything."

"I know," she said, her voice wobbling. "I was just hoping that you were wrong. If he's been stealing valuable coins from Audwin and selling them, he's never going to be able to pay him back or get the coins back." She swallowed. "Audwin will forgive him, I'm sure. I just don't know if Bobby Ray will ever forgive himself."

Jack had wondered that, as well, but knew that was simply going to have to be a bridge they crossed when they came to it.

"Did you find them?" she asked.

"Not the goons, no," he told her. "But I found Mackie. He and I reached an understanding."

"I'm missing a bar of soap," she said. "Did that have anything to do with your *understanding*?" she asked.

"And if it did?"

"Then, good," she said, surprising him. "He deserved it."

"You're bloodthirsty," he said, impressed. "I like that in a woman."

"And I like justice," she said. "And big, badass men like you who aren't afraid to mete it out when needed. You're a good man, Jack Martin."

He swallowed, his throat suddenly tight. "You're a good woman."

She chuckled. "One more lyric and we'll have a country song."

"Smart-ass," he said, laughing.

"You liked my ass last night," she said.

Indeed he did. Heat pooled in his groin, making him shift behind the wheel. "You're just trying to stir me up, aren't you?"

"*Up* works for me," she said, her voice low, almost foggy.

He swerved off the pavement and a car horn blared. *Shit.*

"Jack?" she said, alarmed.

"Mariette, the time for phone sex is not when I'm behind the wheel of my car on eight-five."

She chuckled. "Right. Sorry."

"You don't sound sorry."

"What does sorry sound like?"

"Repentant?"

She *tsked*. "Don't tell me you have the Catholic-schoolgirl fantasy," she said, her voice wicked.

He chuckled darkly. "I will pay you back," he said. "I promise you, I will."

"Can I choose what sort of punishment I want?"

She was killing him. "I'll be there in a few minutes. I'm hanging up now."

"Oooh, are you going to spank me when you get here?"

"Who are you talking to?" He heard his sister ask.

The line instantly went dead.

Jack guffawed.

BOBBY RAY FINISHED LOADING the truck with the delivery for Mariette and, sick with dread, went to let Audwin know he was leaving.

He was absolutely certain that Jack Martin had found the coin and that it was only a matter of time before the police turned up to take him in. He'd re-signed himself to it, even knew he deserved his punishment. He should have never taken anything from Audwin and wished that he could go back and undo it. Audwin had been kind to him and deserved better. Bobby Ray knew he had to be a man about this, had accepted it last night when he'd crawled into the warm bed that Jack Martin had bought for him.

Jack had been right. A good night's sleep, a warm meal and clean clothes had made him feel a lot better. It had given him a chance to clear his head, to come to terms with what he had to do.

When he came back from making this last delivery, he fully intended to tell Audwin what he'd done and then turn himself in. The benefit to serving his time would be that, for the moment anyway, Uncle Mackie wouldn't be able to get to him. Once he got out—he didn't figure they'd keep him in there forever—he'd get as far away from Atlanta as he could. Uncle Mackie was brutal, but ultimately a business-man and pursuing him across the country wouldn't be cost-effective. Had he not been so terrified, that would have occurred to him earlier.

And to be fair, he hadn't wanted to leave Audwin.

Since Martha had passed away, the old man was just as alone and lonely as Bobby Ray had been most of his life. He'd figured they were good for one another and would miss him when he left. He'd miss Prize, too, but the dog would have to stay here.

Bobby Ray could barely feed himself, much less a dog, and Prize deserved better. All of them did.

And a man had to do what a man had to do.

He rounded the corner and watched a familiar car bolt down the driveway, away from the house.

His stomach dropped to his knees and he rushed into the office. "Audwin!"

Bobby Ray ran all over the dairy and even up to the house. It wasn't until he came back to the office that he saw the note in the middle of the desk. "The old man is going to take your punishment until you pay up."

Bobby Ray's knees buckled and he fell to the ground. *No,* he thought. *No, no, no!*

Hands shaking, Bobby Ray reached into his pocket, pulled out a card and dialed the number on the front. Jack Martin answered on the second ring.

"They've taken Audwin," he said, the first tears he'd cried since he was eight years old spilling down his scarred cheeks. "I need your help. I'll do anything," Bobby Ray told him, his voice thick. "Anything you want me to do. Just h-help me," he sobbed.

14

"I DON'T GET IT," Charlie said. "Unless there's some special marking that we're missing this is just an old penny." She looked up at Mariette. "Worth only a penny. Why would Bobby Ray take this?"

Mariette shook her head. "I don't know. Maybe he thought it was worth something. Maybe he knows more about it than we do."

"That's possible," Charlie said. "But I've plugged in all the data from this coin to determine its value and it's worth a penny. If he was expecting some sort of windfall for this, then I'm afraid he's going to be very disappointed."

Charlie's cell suddenly chirped and she checked the display. Her lips curled. "Yes, big brother." Her gaze darted to Mariette. "Yes, she's right here. All right, I will. Keep your panties on." She engaged the speakerphone feature. "There you go," she said. "What's up?"

"Uncle Mackie's goons have Audwin," he said, his tone grim.

Mariette gasped, horrified, and Charlie's eyes rounded and she swore. "Those bastards," she hissed. "What can I do?"

"Charlie, I need every possible address for Mackie and his boys. Even their families. We have to find him quickly."

"I'm on it," Charlie said and quickly set to work, her fingers flying over the keyboard of the laptop.

Mariette's mouth was bone-dry. "You think Mackie ignored your warning?"

"No," he said grimly. "I think this had already been set into motion before I found Mackie. That's what makes this dangerous. He knows that I'm going to come for him, that I'll be gunning for him. And he'll either instruct those morons to dump Audwin off somewhere, or he'll…"

"Or he'll make sure he's never found." The floor shifted beneath her feet.

"How did he find out about the dairy?" Charlie asked without missing a keystroke.

"The goons went through the garbage at the motel looking for Bobby Ray's stuff when he never returned. Geneva, the clerk, didn't pack up Bobby Ray's garbage and evidently there was a check stub from the dairy that had gone into the trash."

"How did you find all of this out?" Mariette wanted to know.

"Bobby Ray called me. He saw them leave and found a note that said Audwin was going to take his punishment until he paid up."

"Where are you headed now?" Charlie asked.

"Back down to the track on the off chance Mackie's still there. Doubtful, I know, but…"

"I'm going to call the office," Charlie said. "And give every available agent an address, Jack. There's too many of them and there's only one of you. Time is of the essence here, so don't argue with me—"

"That's brilliant, Charlie, thanks. Mariette?"

Charlie looked momentarily stunned at her brother's praise, then she smiled wide, went to the landline and called Ranger Security.

"I'm here," she said. "What can I do?"

"I've told Bobby Ray to come down to the shop. He should be there any minute now. I need you to do me a favor."

She swallowed, desperate to have something to do, to have a way to contribute. "Anything."

"He's taken a couple of coins to a pawn shop just outside of Hiram. He's got his tickets, but no money. If you could go pick them up, I'll pay you back. The boy is beside himself, pitiful—" Jack's voice broke. "He's going to pay me back, but in the mean time he needs to be able to give those coins back to Audwin, especially after this. I can't put him through— Do you mind fronting me the—"

"Of course not," she said, a lump swelling in her

throat. Had there ever been a better man? A less self-ish one? Mariette wondered, unbelievably moved by Jack's gesture.

"Tell him I'm texting the list of addresses and where each guy is going," Charlie told her. "I've got seven heading out."

Mariette relayed the information. "I'll get your cell number and text you from my phone so that you'll have mine. Keep me posted, Jack. It's going to be hell not knowing what's going on."

"I will," he said. "Thanks, Mariette."

"Be careful," she said. "It would be terrible if you'd survived Baghdad only to come home and get taken out by a couple of common thugs."

"I'll try not to get whacked," he said, chuckling softly. He swore and she could practically hear his head shaking over the line. "I knew she'd told you about Baghdad."

"Don't be angry at her," she said, crouching low over the phone. "She's proud of you."

"I know that, but she only knows part of the story."

Mariette paused. "Well, when you're ready to share the rest of it then I'm ready to listen."

There was a knock at the back door and Billy Ray poked his head in. His face was wet with tears, his eyes red rimmed, his expression utterly miserable.

"Bobby Ray's here," she said. "Call me when there's news."

"I will."

Mariette disconnected, then stood up and walked over to Bobby Ray. She framed the boy's dear face with her hands and thumbed a tear away, then pressed a kiss to his forehead. "It's going to be all right, Bobby Ray," she said and wrapped her arms around him.

He seemed shocked at first, went completely still as though he wasn't sure what to do—and he probably wasn't, Mariette thought, her heart twisting with agony. God only knew the last time the kid had been properly hugged or shown any sort of affection.

She waited, hoping he'd return the hug and, after the briefest of seconds, she felt him wrap his arms around her, his shoulders shaking with regret. "I'm sorry, Mariette. I'm so, so sorry. I didn't mean to—"

She shushed him, swayed with him back and forth and slid a hand down the back of his head. "It's all right, Bobby Ray. Everybody makes mistakes. You just got into something you couldn't find a way out of on your own. But you've got friends. You've got people who care about you. You can ask for help if you need it. There's no shame in that." She drew back and drew a bracing breath. "Now let's go get those coins back, shall we?"

"It's a lot of money, Mariette." He swallowed, clearly humbled. "I can't believe he's going to do this for me, let me pay him back. Mr. Martin is a good guy, isn't he?"

Mariette smiled up at him. "He's the best."

And as much as it was hard to believe, given how long she'd known him…he unequivocally owned her heart.

How in the hell had that happened?

Hiatus, her ass. She'd gone and fallen in love with him.

JUST AS HE'D FIGURED, Mackie had left the track and gone to ground. Jack had checked in with everyone else and so far none of them had had any luck, either. Payne had checked Goon One's home address, McCann had taken Goon Two's and Jamie had started working the family angle.

It was amazing how many of these men, when faced with any sort of fear or threat, returned to their first form of refuge—behind their mother's skirts. Which was why Jack had decided to take a little trip over to Uncle Mackie's mother's house. The address Charlie had found for the woman was in an affluent neighborhood, one of those gated communities with its own clubhouse and swimming pool.

He circled the block, noting a red sports car tucked all the way in the back, parked at an angle that had practically hidden it from view.

But it was Uncle Mackie's.

The vanity plate read Bet Me.

A slow, lethal smile slid across Jack's lips as he

pulled his truck up far enough to nudge the little car's bumper. The fiberglass gave a gratifying crack.

That felt good.

Nailing that fat bastard to the wall was going to feel better. Evidently hearing the noise, Mackie raced outside, took one look at Jack and darted back into the house like a mole returning to its hole.

Shit. He was going to have to abandon good manners.

He bolted for the door, knocked twice and then let himself inside. A petite woman with gray hair and the straightest backbone Jack had ever seen suddenly blocked his path.

"Can I help you?" she said archly.

"I need to speak to your son, ma'am."

She poked her finger in his chest. "Now you listen here," she said. "I don't allow any of that damned fool betting business in my house. If you've got an issue with my son, then you need to take it up at the track. But it doesn't come here."

"Then he shouldn't," Jack told her. "He's taken an old man hostage and, forgive me, ma'am, but I'm not leaving here without getting the necessary information I need to get him back from your son."

She quailed, then rallied, fire lighting her gaze and she whirled around. "Morris!" she called threateningly.

Morris? Jack heard the front door slam and took off. Mackie had barely taken five steps before Jack vaulted from the porch and launched himself at him, pinning him to the ground. Jack pulled a gun from his waistband, disengaged the safety and pressed it to the back of Mackie's head.

"You have to the count of five," Jack told him, "and then I'm going to blow your brains out through your face."

"You wouldn't, not in front of my mother," Mackie said, though he didn't sound altogether certain.

"One."

"Mom!" he called frantically, trying to dislodge Jack. "Mommy!" he squealed.

"Two."

"Go ahead and shoot him," Mackie's mother said, shooting Jack a wink that her son couldn't see. "But do me a favor and drag him around back. I don't want a mess in the front yard."

"Mom! No, please. Mom!"

"Three."

"I didn't know!" Mackie screamed frantically. "The two jackasses took it upon themselves! I didn't tell them to do it!"

"Four."

"He's in the trunk of my car!" Mackie wailed. "I didn't know what to do— I needed to be able to think— I—"

White-hot anger burst through Jack and he flipped him over and planted his fist into Mackie's nose, then reached down and withdrew his car keys from his pocket.

Mackie's mother's face was stark white. "You've put an old man into your trunk and brought him here? He's been in your car the whole time?" She took her shoe off and proceeded to pummel the hell out of him right there on the front lawn, Mackie rolling and writhing beneath the blows, trying to get away from her.

Heart pounding so hard he felt nauseous, Jack hurried around back and hit the truck release button on the keyless remote. It popped, but didn't open completely. A flannel-covered arm popped up and pushed at it.

"Audwin!" Jack hollered. "Are you all right?"

Audwin glared up at him. "I was better until you rammed the back of his car."

Jack grabbed the older man's hand and helped him awkwardly out of the trunk. "Did they hurt you?"

"No," he said. "Just got the jump on me was all," he told him, clearly embarrassed. "Nasty characters, though," he said. "I'll admit I was worried there for a while. Those big bastards thought their boss would be happy that they'd nabbed me. But you'd gotten a hold of him first and put the fear into him. He didn't know what to do with me, so he had those assholes throw me into the back of his car."

"But you're not hurt?"

"Only my pride, boy, and I reckon that'll survive." He looked up sharply. "How's Bobby Ray?" He shook his head. "If he'd only told me what was going on, I could have helped the boy. I'd have given him the money to pay them off," he said. "He wouldn't have had to take those damned coins."

Jack blinked. "You knew about the coins?"

"Not until I heard them talking about it. They were planning on going back and tearing my place apart to look for them." His lips twisted. "They weren't going to tell their boss about that, either."

"He's gone to get the coins out of hock," Jack told him. "And Mariette found the other one in a block of butter she'd taken up to her apartment. You'll get them all back, Audwin." He paused. "I'd appreciate if you'd cut the boy some slack on this. He's spent so long between a rock and a hard place he doesn't know what a soft one feels like."

Audwin scowled at him. "You think I don't know that?" He shook his head. "I don't know why he thought they were valuable," he said. "I'm not an official collector. Those are just pieces that have been given to me by family members—my dad and grandfather, mostly. I've always had a knack for finding pennies after losing people, you know. Everyone thinks that's an old wives' tale, but I'm here to tell you that it's not. I've been finding them since I was a boy. I found several after my daddy died. It's supposed to be their way of letting you know they're okay, you know? That you can let them go. I've found half a dozen since Martha died, two of them right there on her headstone."

Jack had never heard that before, but was never one to doubt or question the unexplained.

"You mean you didn't know some of the coins were valuable?"

He shook his head, clearly puzzled. "I had no idea. They were keepsakes, not cash."

Bobby Ray had gotten extremely lucky. "Come on," Jack told him. "I'll take you home."

He called Mariette first. "I've got him and he's fine. Tell Charlie so she can call everyone else off."

"I will," she said. He heard her relay the news to Bobby Ray and the boy's sigh of relief was loud enough that he heard it over the line.

"And you took care of the other?"

"I did. He has them and is going to leave here right now and go put them back where they came from."

Jack darted a look at Audwin from the corner of his eye. "He knows," he said. "But I don't think he's going to let on."

"Good," Mariette said. "I think that would be for the best." She paused. "I'll see you soon."

It was almost, but not quite, a question, and he suddenly realized that she must think that because this case was closed, they were finished, as well. That he would just pack up his things and move on with his life as though she'd been a mere distraction, a fun little excursion on this assignment.

Nothing could be further from the truth.

And no one was more surprised by that than Jackson Oak Martin.

"You will," he promised.

CHARLIE HUGGED MARIETTE's neck and gave her a squeeze. "I'll see you soon," she said. "I've enjoyed being down here with you. As far as assignments go, short of the one where I met my husband, this one has been the best."

Mariette grinned at her. "I'm glad to hear it."

Charlie hesitated. "He's crazy about you, you know."

Mariette's gaze flew to hers. "What? Who?"

"Don't play coy," she said. "You think I didn't know what was going on from the moment the two of you laid eyes on each other?"

Mariette blushed. "Charlie, I—"

"See?" she said, laughing softly. "I can't even bring him up without your face turning six shades of red. And Livvie's got it right. You do look gooey. She told me so earlier today."

"Gooey?"

"Like the middle part of the brownie," Charlie told her. "Warm and gooey and good."

She certainly felt like the middle part of the brownie when she was with Jack, that was for damned sure. Except for when she wasn't wound tight with desire, a desperate throbbing nerve of need.

She'd never felt this way before, Mariette thought. She never needed, admired or craved a man the way she did Jack Martin. Was he handsome? Certainly. Hot? Most definitely. But he was so much more than that. He was a man who cared enough about the happiness of a less-fortunate boy that he'd done everything he could possibly do to pave an easier way for him. That took character, it took heart, it took…a real man.

Charlie gave her another squeeze. "I'd better go," she said, her eyes twinkling. "I'd hate to delay your spanking."

And with that parting comment, she turned and walked away.

Mariette looked around her suddenly empty shop and felt an odd pang. For the first time in her life she wasn't quite sure what to do with herself.

Thankfully, she didn't have an opportunity to dwell on that, because Jack chose that moment to stroll into the shop. The bell above the door jingled, signaling his arrival and there was something almost providential in the ring this time. Something that made her smile.

He strolled determinedly to her, then wrapped her in his arms and kissed her. He breathed her in, savored her mouth, tangled his tongue around hers as though somehow the act seemed to trigger a reset button, a way to get back to who they were.

"I have some bad news," Jack told her, pulling back to stare into her face. His gaze was soft and tender, his blue eyes rife with an emotion she hadn't seen in a long, long time.

"What's that?"

"I'm not going to be run off as easily as Nathaniel," he said. "In the first place, you'd have to find somebody bigger and, short of the real Jolly Green Giant, I don't think that's going to happen. In the second place, I'm not as easily intimidated and have a thicker head than anyone you've likely ever gotten involved with before."

Mariette blinked up at him and smiled. "What gave you the idea I wanted to get rid of you?"

"Nothing yet," he told her. "I'm just making a pre-emptive strike. Letting you know where I stand." He paused. "Where do *I* stand, Mariette?"

On the threshold of her heart, Mariette thought. And she had no doubt that he would knock and pummel and batter the door down until she let him in.

"With me," she said simply. "I don't know what this is," she admitted. "And don't have the experience to know what should happen next. All I know is that I want to be with you. As much as possible, whenever possible."

He nuzzled the side of her neck. "That can certainly be arranged."

"Your sister knows about us," Mariette told him.

He chuckled. "I never doubted it. That's why she filled your ears full. She didn't want you toying with my affections."

She blinked up at him. "What?"

"Charlie's protective," he said. He swallowed. "And I wasn't myself when I came home. I... I lost a couple of men. In Baghdad. I'm sure she told you that."

Mariette squeezed him. "She did. I'm so sorry, Jack."

His gaze turned inward, reliving a nightmare she couldn't see. "It was hell," he said. "But there was this one guy, Johnson... I really liked him. He was young and smart." He released a breath. "Bobby Ray actually reminds me of him. They have that same spirit of goodness, you know?"

She nodded.

"Anyway, when the blast hit he'd been talking about what he wanted out of a woman," Jack told her. He shook his head. "One of the other guys had just made some jackass comment about—" He blinked. "Never mind what it was about. But Johnson's reply was wholesome, innocent. He just wanted a woman who knew how to cook." His gaze tangled with hers. "And then I found you."

"Oh, Jack," she said, her heart crowding into her throat.

"He died in my arms, Mariette, and as horrible as that was, he kept trying to tell me something before he died. He was shouting it. He grabbed me and shook me and repeated himself until he couldn't anymore. And I couldn't hear him."

Oh, Lord…

Because of his ear. No doubt the force of the blast had rendered him temporarily deaf and… She swallowed, held him closer.

"I can see his face, every move of his lips— everything about that few minutes—plain as day. But I still haven't been able to figure out what he was trying to tell me. And it was important, Mariette. He spent his last breath trying to share it with me." He paused again, looked down and his tortured gaze tangled with hers. "I've been taking lip-reading lessons trying to learn the technique so that I can figure it out."

She blinked, astonished. "You have?"

"It was important to him, whatever it was. I need to pass the message along."

So simple and yet so profound. Sweet heaven, had there ever been a better man? "Have you made any headway on it yet?"

"Just a little." He glanced down at her. "It's much more difficult than I'd anticipated. For instance, 'I love you' could easily be mistaken for 'olive juice' or 'elephant shoes.' See, give it a go. I'll mouth it and you try to guess which one of those phrases I said."

She nodded. "Okay."

She watched his lips, her heart beating strangely in her chest. He did it and she stared at him, completely at a loss. He was right. He could have said any one of those lines. "Olive juice," she guessed.

"No," he told her, dragging her closer to him. "I said 'I love you.'"

"Oh."

"On purpose, Mariette," he said. "You think I'm insane, don't you?"

Mariette didn't know that this much happiness could occupy a single body, let alone hers. She flushed with joy, felt it permeate every cell, making her glow inside.

"Then I'm going crazy with you," she said, lifting up on tiptoe to give him a kiss. She drew back once more, framed his dear face and slid her thumb along his jaw. "It wasn't your fault, Jack," she said.

He frowned at her, a line wrinkling his brow.

"Baghdad." It might not be her place, but dammit, he needed to hear it. "It wasn't your fault."

He went chalk white and staggered back against the display case.

"Jack?"

"Say that again," he said, his gaze fastening on her mouth.

"It's not your fault, Jack."

Jack passed a hand over his face, his big body trembling. A dry bark of laugher erupted from his throat and he shook his head, but he wasn't amused. She didn't know exactly what he was, but...

"That's what he said," Jack murmured. "All this time I've been worried about making sure his message was delivered and it was for me," he said, his voice cracking. "'It's not your fault, Oak,'" he'd said. He glanced up at her. "That's what they called me. Mighty Oak, actually. It's my middle name."

Tears burned the backs of her lids and blurred her vision. "I know. Your sister told me."

He rolled his eyes, snorted. "Of course she did. The little blabbermouth."

She rained gentle kisses on his face. "Yes, but you olive juice her."

He chuckled weakly. "I do," he said. "And I olive juice you, too." He threaded his fingers through hers and then tugged her toward the staircase. "Come on," he told her. "I believe I owe you a spanking."

That he did, Mariette thought. And she'd happily take her punishment for as long as he'd dole it out.

And she hoped that was forever.

Epilogue

One month later...

THE SURGEON WALKED INTO the waiting room and said, "Bishop family," in carrying tones.

Five former Army Rangers, a pregnant security agent, a dairy farmer, a girl with Down syndrome decked out in Hello Kitty attire and a pastry chef all stood.

The surgeon's eyes widened at the imposing, eclectic group.

Audwin stepped forward. "How's my son?"

The surgeon smiled. "He came through with flying colors, sir. I'm confident that this surgery will smooth out those scars and make him feel much more confident in his appearance. He's in recovery now and will be moved to a room—"

"A private room," Payne interjected. "On my wing."

Payne's wing was actually labor and delivery, but the surgeon knew better than to argue with him, Mariette thought, smiling as she and Jack shared a look.

"As you wish, Mr. Payne," he said. "It'll probably be a little while before he's awake. I'll have someone notify you when we move him."

Everyone breathed a collective sigh of relief. It hadn't taken much to convince Bobby Ray to have the corrective surgery to repair his face. What he'd balked at was the cost, but Audwin had insisted that he couldn't think of a better way to spend his money. He'd sold every coin worth any value, had only kept the ones he'd found on Martha's headstone.

Bobby Ray had moved in with Audwin and the change in the boy since being taken under the older man's wing—and that of all the rest of them—was nothing short of phenomenal. He planned to start taking college classes in the fall, once he'd finished healing.

Jack, meanwhile, had moved in with Mariette and home had never felt so right. She went to bed with him snuggled up to her back and woke up in the same fashion. She felt cherished and appreciated and generally adored, and there was nothing quite so wonderful than being unconditionally loved.

She squeezed his hand, looked up at him and smiled. "Olive juice," she said, saying it for the first time so that he could hear her. The emotions were there, but for whatever reason, the words had been more difficult to say.

But she needed to say them and, more importantly, he needed to hear them.

He grinned, bent down and pressed a kiss to her lips. "Olive juice you, too, sweetheart."

Charlie shot them both a perplexed look and rolled her eyes. "The inside jokes are getting a little old," she said. "Olive juice? What does that even mean?"

Jack tugged Mariette up against his side and gave her a squeeze. "It means we're happy."

Yes, Mariette thought. That, and so much more.

* * * * *

PASSION

For a spicier, decidedly hotter read—
this is your destination for romance!

COMING NEXT MONTH
AVAILABLE FEBRUARY 28, 2012

#669 TIME OUT
Jill Shalvis

#670 ONCE A HERO...
Uniformly Hot!
Jillian Burns

#671 HAVE ME
It's Trading Men!
Jo Leigh

#672 TAKE IT DOWN
Island Nights
Kira Sinclair

#673 BLAME IT ON THE BACHELOR
All the Groom's Men
Karen Kendall

#674 THE PLAYER'S CLUB: FINN
The Player's Club
Cathy Yardley

You can find more information on upcoming Harlequin® titles,
free excerpts and more at www.HarlequinInsideRomance.com.

HBCNM0212

REQUEST YOUR FREE BOOKS!
2 FREE NOVELS PLUS 2 FREE GIFTS!

red-hot reads!

HBI1B

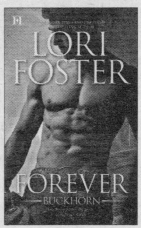

New York Times *and* USA TODAY *bestselling author*
Maya Banks presents book three in her miniseries
PREGNANCY & PASSION.

TEMPTED BY HER INNOCENT KISS

Available March 2012 from Harlequin Desire!

There came a time in a man's life when he knew he was well and truly caught. Devon Carter stared down at the diamond ring nestled in velvet and acknowledged that this was one such time. He snapped the lid closed and shoved the box into the breast pocket of his suit.

He had two choices. He could marry Ashley Copeland and fulfill his goal of merging his company with Copeland Hotels, thus creating the largest, most exclusive line of resorts in the world, or he could refuse and lose it all.

Put in that light, there wasn't much he could do except pop the question.

The doorman to his Manhattan high-rise apartment hurried to open the door as Devon strode toward the street. He took a deep breath before ducking into his car, and the driver pulled into traffic.

Tonight was the night. All of his careful wooing, the countless dinners, kisses that started brief and casual and became more breathless—all a lead-up to tonight. Tonight his seduction of Ashley Copeland would be complete, and then he'd ask her to marry him.

He shook his head as the absurdity of the situation hit him for the hundredth time. Personally, he thought William Copeland was crazy for forcing his daughter down Devon's throat.

Ashley was a sweet enough girl, but Devon had no desire

to marry anyone.

William had other plans. He'd told Devon that Ashley had no head for the family business. She was too softhearted, too naive. So he'd made Ashley part of the deal. The catch? Ashley wasn't to know of it. Which meant Devon was stuck playing stupid games.

Ashley was supposed to think this was a grand love match. She was a starry-eyed woman who preferred her animal-rescue foundation over board meetings, charts and financials for Copeland Hotels.

If she ever found out the truth, she wouldn't take it well.

And hell, he couldn't blame her.

But no matter the reason for his proposal, before the night was over, she'd have no doubts that she belonged to him.

What will happen when Devon marries Ashley?
Find out in Maya Banks's passionate new novel
TEMPTED BY HER INNOCENT KISS
Available March 2012 from Harlequin Desire!